THE
ENDANGEREDS

HarperCollinsChildren'sBooks

PHILIPPE COUSTEAU
AND AUSTIN ASLAN

HARPER
An Imprint of HarperCollins*Publishers*

The Endangereds #1

www.harpercollinschildrens.com

Library of Congress Cataloging-in-Publication Data

Names: Cousteau, Philippe, author. | Aslan, Austin, author.
Title: The Endangereds / Philippe Cousteau with Austin Aslan.
Description: First edition. | New York : Harper, [2020] | Series:
Endangereds ; #1 | Audience: Ages 8-12. | Audience: Grades 4-6. |
Summary: Nukilik, a polar bear, joins Wangari, a pangolin with a genius for engineering, Murdock, an extremely sarcastic narwhal, and Arief, an orangutan with a big dream, to safeguard other endangered animals.
Identifiers: LCCN 2020008866 | ISBN 978-0-06-289416-8 (hardcover)
Subjects: CYAC: Endangered species—Fiction. | Animal rescue—Fiction.
Classification: LCC PZ7.1.C6832 End 2020 | DDC [Fic]—dc23
LC record available at https://lccn.loc.gov/2020008866

Typography by Corina Lupp
20 21 22 23 24 PC/LSCH 10 9 8 7 6 5 4 3 2 1
❖
First Edition

To my daughter, Vivienne Antoinette Cousteau.
You inspire me every day to laugh more, love more,
and ask more questions. This book is for you; I hope
that in some small way it will help to build a better
world for you to inherit.
—Philippe Cousteau

To my dad, Gary, who took me camping, hiking,
and fishing every chance he got and taught me to cherish
the Great Outdoors. That epic trek into Oak Creek
Canyon shaped me more than you'll ever know.
—Austin Aslan

CHAPTER ONE

NUKILIK

(Ursus maritimus)

The shore was too far away.

The polar bear leaned forward and gazed out across the Great Ocean. The mass of snow-patched land that was her home was half a day's march from here—or it would be if the ice bridge hadn't melted.

She tensed. Swimming that distance would take great strength, possibly more than she had.

A voice snapped her from her thoughts. "Stay back from the edge, Nukilik. The ice could break away under your weight. You're not a cub anymore."

“I know, Mother.”

“Oh, I’m ‘Mother’ now? What happened to Mamma?”

Nukilik huffed her annoyance. She was starting to understand why bears her age usually struck off on their own. “I’m not a cub anymore, remember?”

Nukilik was ready, she thought, to leave Mother’s side. According to The Ways, it was time. But Nukilik could not set out to explore the Great Realm alone right now. She and her mother were trapped on a drifting island of ice, starving and weak, growing weaker.

Hunger gnawed at her belly.

The bears had waited days for the ice sheet to drift toward land or for a bridge of ice to refreeze. But it was too warm. Based on where the day star rose and set and the length of the nights with their green-ribbon displays, she and Mother should have been safe venturing so far out over the ice to find food.

They had gone out. But they never found food. And now they were cut off from home and Nukilik’s tongue was salty and dry.

“We should just swim for it.”

“We need a plan, Nuk.”

"We've already waited too long!" Nukilik grumbled. "You should have listened to me the first day the ice broke."

Mother sighed. "You don't think I've been on drifting ice islands before? But they never went out to sea like this. Everything is changing."

Nukilik knew her mother was not to blame for their worrisome situation, but she wasn't going to admit it.

"The knowledge of how things work is stored in our bones," Mother explained. "It was put in you when you were still inside of me. We're taught The Ways by the Old Natures who watch over the Realm as stars now. But The Ways have gone awry."

Nukilik scanned the distance, looking for icebergs they might reach. Her stomach growled. Then Mother's stomach growled too, as if their tummies were having a conversation of their own. The polar bears shared an irritated look and then both of them managed a laugh.

There was nothing funny about any of this, but at least they had each other.

"Mother, look!" Nukilik pointed to a strange object floating on the water far away. Its shape was too regular to be an iceberg. Nukilik had seen human vessels before, always at a distance, but never one quite like this.

"That's a human ship," Mother told her. "I never used to see them, but they're appearing more and more."

Nukilik had so many questions about the humans. But she didn't voice them aloud. Her mother would only say, "Just keep away from them, Nuk. They're dangerous." That was her way of not having to admit that she didn't know anything about them either.

The ship slowly disappeared from sight. The day star touched down beneath the waters and nighttime spread. The Old Natures, twinkling through the green ribbons, looked down at the uncertain polar bears but offered them no help.

The moon had not yet risen, but the shore was easy to make out as a dark silhouette wedged between the starlit sky and the green reflections on the water. Land appeared farther away than ever.

Nukilik did not know if she could swim long enough to reach home. But she was sure that if they didn't try soon, she and Mother would perish either way.

CHAPTER TWO

NUKILIK

(Ursus maritimus)

"What's the deal here?" someone squawked. Nukilik blinked away the dawn light and zeroed in on the figure of a puffin bird perched on the edge of the ice. Its big beak had colorful stripes. "You two making a break for the Bahamas?"

Nukilik glanced at her mother, who was ignoring the bird but eyeing Nukilik sternly. *You know the rules*, that face said. *We're predators. We don't speak to other species.*

Nukilik stretched awake. With a certain rebellious glee, she ignored her mother's look. "What's a bahama?" she asked the puffin.

Somewhat surprised, the puffin was delighted to engage in conversation. "A Caribbean island, I think."

Nukilik could suddenly appreciate the wisdom of her mother's rule. "Okay, but what's a caribbean?" she asked, avoiding her mother's unhappy glower.

"You'll have to ask a long-distance tern what caribbeans are. The point is they're *waaay* far south. You'll find out yourself if you stay on this floater much longer!" The puffin scratched an itch with its large rainbow-splashed beak. "Listen, the current's pulling strong to the south. You two had better bail if you plan on seeing home again. The ice sheet won't refreeze this year."

"How do you know that?" Nukilik demanded.

"The humans along the bay are already playing in the water. That's saying something. The winter's done."

Nukilik didn't know what the bird was talking about. She was overcome with curiosity. "You've seen humans? Tell me more about them."

The puffin shrugged. "A bizarre bunch. You're better off ignoring them."

The bird's advice sounded awfully similar to what Nukilik's mother would say. This annoyed Nuk, and her stomach grumbled. The puffin heard the low protest and wisely hopped backward a step. The polar bear's muscles tightened with readiness. Could she spring on the know-it-all bird without making a fool of herself or cracking the ice?

Too late to find out. Something about Nukilik's posture or expression spooked the bird. The puffin took to the air and never looked back.

"As predators, we don't talk to other species," her mother emphasized. "They don't make any sense, especially the birds. Why don't you listen to me anymore? Why won't you honor The Ways?"

Nukilik felt a flash of anger heat up her neck. "What Ways, Mother? All the rules have changed."

Mother did not respond for a long time. When she finally spoke, she said, "I'm very hungry. And weak. I know you are too. But we can't keep waiting. You were right, Nuk. We should have acted sooner. It's time to swim."

Nukilik sensed an emotion that polar bears rarely feel; she was afraid.

Mother rose on shaky legs and stepped forward toward the edge of the berg. It was thin out near the water, but she did not fall through. She had become too skinny and light within her wrinkled fur coat to crack the ice. Nukilik joined her, and together, the polar bears entered the ocean and began to swim toward the distant shores.

Nukilik could sense the vastness of the blue depths beneath her. She imagined losing her grip on the surface, the abyss pulling her down. The fear of falling into the black depths fueled her final reserves of strength.

For a long, long time Nuk knew nothing but the motions of her legs reaching toward home, pushing through cold water with her paws. She ducked her head underwater occasionally, to see if any kind of meal might be passing below. There was nothing within reach. Her exhaustion came and went, but she could not stop. When Mother spied a tiny iceberg to rest upon, they swam toward it and climbed aboard. The warmth of the day star dried Nukilik's blondish-white fur and made her feel relaxed.

"I'm sleepy," she admitted.

"Don't go to sleep," her mother insisted. "You might not wake up."

Nukilik felt a chill that had nothing to do with the cool breeze.

She had once seen another bear fall into the forever sleep, his nature leaving his flesh behind to rise into the night to be with the old ones. Nuk was not yet ready or willing for her nature to leave the ground. But she was so tired. Maybe it wouldn't be that bad. "If The Ways are failing us," she suggested, "maybe it's time our natures rose above the green ribbons."

"That's your exhaustion talking, love," warned Mother. "Take heart and have faith. I named you Nukilik because your nature is strong. You were made with a great purpose in mind."

Mother's expression was so certain and confident that Nukilik couldn't look away.

"We should move on," said Mother.

They slipped back into the water and continued paddling toward home.

Nukilik kept her eyes on the shore, which did not seem to be growing nearer. But as twilight gathered in the sky, the shadows changed. The land suddenly appeared within reach.

"Almost there. We can do this," Mother encouraged, speaking between deep breaths. "Maybe we can find a meal before dark!"

Nukilik felt encouraged by her mother's reassurances. The young polar bear was staring at the shore, which had easy landings on either side of a jutting cliff face. She opened her mouth to ask Mother which shore they should aim for but was surprised by a sudden racket on the water's surface. They were swimming straight into an oncoming pod of bowhead whales!

The bowheads breached in waves and blew plumes of mist out of their blowholes. They were moving quickly. Nukilik saw why. She gasped and almost choked on the water and sea foam churned up by the activity: the human ship they had seen in the distance a day earlier was chasing the whales. Up close, it was enormous, and moving fast. Several humans were leaning over the edges of the ship, making excited noises and pointing at the water.

Nukilik scanned the surface for her mother but could not find her among the commotion. "Mamma!" she cried out. "Mamma, where are you?"

Amid all the splashing and turmoil, no answer came.

Nukilik dodged the breaching whales as they rushed forward. The ship was almost upon her. If it hit her, she would drown. She swam at a sprint, finding extra strength she didn't know she had. She paddled fiercely, feeling the pull of the water as the giant human vessel powered forward, its undertow dragging her toward it. The ship spat up foamy water as it rushed past. Nukilik tumbled in the wake, struggling to stay above the surface.

The waters calmed. Straggling bowheads raced to catch the rest of their pod. Nukilik paddled in place, circling. "Mamma! Mamma, I'm over here."

She couldn't find her mother. She called and called, but no reply came. Exhausted, she abandoned her search and made her way toward the nearest beach. She was sure Mamma would be there waiting for her.

Eventually, she made landfall and crawled onto solid ground, weary beyond any experience she'd known. She lumbered up a gently sloping shore of polished black rocks. It felt as if she were climbing a mountain.

"Mamma!"

She called out again and again. "Mamma!"

The snow had melted away here, and Nukilik felt

exposed and vulnerable without her natural ability to blend into her background. Even now, in the dim twilight of this season's night, she knew she glowed against the landscape. She fought the realization, but it settled upon her anyway: if Mamma were here, they'd be able to spot each other.

"She came ashore on the other beach," Nukilik told herself.

She looked up at the tall crags of the land formation that jutted out into the water, cutting her off from the other shore. She was too exhausted to go farther.

"We'll meet up in the morning, Mamma."

She shook herself off and curled up at the top of the pebbly beach, ready to sleep. She knew she might not wake up. But if this was her last night on the ground before her nature went to be among her ancestors circling above, then maybe that would be all right.

She refused to listen to a voice in her head warning her that Mamma might already be there, looking down.

CHAPTER THREE

NUKILIK

(Ursus maritimus)

Nukilik awoke with the day star rising in the sky, stiff and weak and cold. She slowly took to her haunches while stretching and looked back out on the Great Ocean and felt afraid and alone.

"Mamma!" she cried, looking back and forth between the waters and the cliff.

A deep, painful hunger pulled at her gut. She knew she didn't have the energy to climb the steep, rocky formations. She didn't think she could swim around them either. Her choices were to wait here for Mamma to come to her or to set out to find her using the long way around, walking inland for a while before trekking up the hillside through the boulders.

A scent was on the air: humans. The smell that reached her nose came from somewhere beyond the rocky crags hugging the shore behind her, and it conjured up a strong association with the ship that had torn her mother away from her.

But the smell smacked of something else too: food. Nukilik needed to eat to have strength to search for Mamma. She rose to investigate. Stumbling and staggering, she forced herself up along the crags and followed the land around a hill patched with snow until she spotted the source of the smells in the distance.

In spite of her raging hunger, she waited and watched. She remembered what the puffin bird had said about humans as she studied the curious, colorful domes erected on the bare ground partway along a pebbly beach. Strewn about were bizarre items that the bear could not begin to categorize. But no humans appeared.

A gust of wind brought with it a strong scent of food. Nukilik could no longer resist. She set out across the barren rock toward the dome dwelling. The nearer she got, the stronger the smells became and the less cautious she grew.

The food was inside the dome. Nuk tore into the fabric structure. She poked her head and front legs inside and felt warm air. Her eyes were flooded by an array of strange, colorful objects. Her snout immediately zeroed in on an open metal container containing many smaller containers. She dove at the objects, scattering them about. She tore at them and bit into them and was rewarded most of the time with . . . food!

She cut her tongue on the sharp edges of one of the smaller containers, but she hardly cared. She wiggled her way entirely inside the dome and sat upright, sniffing and licking and chewing and devouring. The tastes were sweet and savory. Some were bitter or acidic. But her stomach began to fill.

I'll bring Mamma here, she thought. *She can have her fill too, once I find her.*

She gnawed the lid off a big vat and found a creamy, sticky food inside. She shoved her snout into the opening and gobbled up as much of the substance as she could reach. Her hunger began to go away. She pulled her face back and stuffed her paw into the container to scoop out more of the mucky food. But once her paw was inside, she couldn't get it back out.

The polar bear shook her limb vigorously. She pulled awkwardly out of the dome and tripped over a box. She sat up and gnawed at the container jamming her paw.

The bark of a human startled her.

On top of a small hill, two humans stood watching her, each perfectly balanced on their hind legs. They had fur only on top of their heads but were covered in colorful wrappings everywhere below their faces. They pointed and vocalized. They grew quiet when Nukilik noticed them.

"Hello, polar bear!" The female human lifted a forelimb and shook it in the air. "I guess you like peanut butter! You look very hungry. Keep it!"

Humans are always barking, thought Nukilik. These two—one female and one a slightly taller male—would make a very good meal, once she managed to tear off their wrappings.

"Can we help you free your paw from the jar?" the

male barked. He slowly began to approach. The female followed him.

The polar bear was impressed with their bravery. She remained still but alert.

"You're starving, aren't you?" The female expressed concern. "You poor thing."

The male human drew nearer and stopped within reach. Nukilik struggled with a sudden urge to attack. She was so hungry.

"Don't be alarmed," vocalized the male, reaching out his forelimbs. "So gorgeous. I'm just gonna grab the tub and give it a yank. If you stick around, Dr. Fellows might share some of the fish we just netted."

The male inched forward, cautiously extending his furless paw. He touched her arm. Nukilik growled.

The human jerked back but stayed his ground. The bear relaxed with a gruff snort. The male moved forward again, grasped either side of the container, and tugged.

The object came free and the male stumbled but stayed upright. So strange how they could stand like that. "It worked!" he barked.

Nukilik licked her paw covered in the creamy tan food. *Mother will like this stuff.*

"Gooding. Out of the way!" The bark had come from the female who was now standing near the dome.

"Doc, it's okay. Look. She's not dangerous. We already helped her get—"

"She ate all the medicine," the female human called over. "We don't have a way to pump her stomach. She'll die without an evac. We have a permit to extract a bear. This young female might as well be it."

The male turned and considered Nukilik with a sympathetic stare. "Looks like you chose us, gal."

The female human grasped a long pole in her paws and held it level, pointing it at Nukilik. Instinctively, Nuk knew it was a dangerous boom stick. She'd heard stories about them. She leaped up and bounded away, almost running over the male. Nukilik stumbled and landed heavily. She stopped after a few more lumbering steps. She was too tired to run. Her stomach was hurting again all of a sudden. But the pain wasn't hunger.

What's happening? she thought. *I need to find Mamma.*

A boom, like nearby thunder, cracked over the Realm.

Nukilik felt a sudden, fierce sting on her neck. She brushed uselessly at something lodged in her fur, then reared up on her hind legs and bellowed, lashing out at the air. The male human scrambled backward. Nukilik cried out one last time then collapsed to the ground.

She grew impossibly tired. Surely this had to be the start of the forever sleep. *I'm going above, to the green ribbons.* She wasn't afraid. Her chin sank and rested on the gravel. *Maybe now I'll find my purpose, Mamma. I'll keep watch over you and the others who are left.*

CHAPTER FOUR

NUKILIK

(Ursus maritimus)

Nukilik's body did not settle into the forever sleep that morning, but the following days and weeks were confusing. Her waking moments were sluggish. She would think about her mother and panic, growing dizzy and angry. And then a sting would come to her neck or shoulder, and she would fall back asleep. She had memories of eating, of being strapped firmly to a flat surface and poked with sharp objects, and of being watched by humans who paced back and forth and vocalized affectionately. How could they speak so sweetly when they were treating her so harshly?

Sometimes she saw the female who had pointed the boom stick. "I need to know if Mamma's okay," Nukilik tried to tell her. But she couldn't decipher the meaning of their constant utterances, and the humans clearly didn't understand her either.

During this time she was in a strange cave—a closed space—but couldn't make sense of it. The walls and ceiling and floor were too regular, forming perfect geometric shapes. And this cave vibrated, tilted, swooned, and rocked, providing her with an uncomfortable sense of motion that she could not track with her eyes.

And then all the moving and traveling stopped. Nukilik awoke in a strangely tiny canyon with no exit. She believed at first that she was somewhere back in the Great Realm. It smelled weird, and the air was warm, and there were bright points of light high overhead that were not the day star, the moon, or the Old Natures. But everything vaguely felt like home.

As she explored, though, she came to realize that

nothing here was natural and all of it had been designed on purpose to trap her.

The humans made this place and put me here, she sensed with gathering unease.

She picked out details as she struggled to make sense of it all. High above the canyon walls, the sky was shut out by a looming, dome-shaped barrier made of an odd material that looked like sheets of ice but was too clear and regularly shaped. The bright points of light hung from the ceiling of this dome. Giant fake rocks ran up one of the high walls. She could climb the rock structures, but she still couldn't reach the top of the canyon. A third of the enclosure was taken up by a deep channel filled with cold, flowing salt water. The water entered through slats in one wall and exited through slats in the opposite wall.

She wanted to learn what was beyond the enclosure's rims. It was obvious that a larger world existed beneath the strange, looming dome, but she was in a hole and couldn't glimpse beyond the lips of her pit.

Once every few days, after she ate the food that mysteriously appeared among the rocks, she would become drowsy and collapse into a half sleep. This was when the humans would cart her into a closed room and put her on a table and strap her down and poke her sluggish body.

If she ever got ahold of a human, she would let it know how she felt about being locked up here.

Her starving body slowly gathered strength. She swam in the pool to bathe and to take her mind off her hopelessness. She found a kind of fake bone on the floor of the pool. It must have been put here by the humans, and though it wasn't as good as the real thing, she couldn't help but gnaw it broodingly whenever she thought of her mother.

One day she thought she glimpsed a narwhal watching her beyond the upstream slats. *I'm hallucinating about home*, she thought. She swam to the slats in the wall to investigate. The water of the open blue beyond smelled of narwhal, but she saw nothing alive.

Several minutes later as she sat near the water drying, a narwhal *did* appear at the gate. Its long, straight tusk poked through the bars.

"Knock, knock," it said.

Nukilik and the small whale watched each other.

She knew better than to start a conversation with it. Narwhals were known to be whimsical and offensive. She and her mother had tasted one once—it had washed up on the beach. Nuk recalled it as the worst meal she'd ever had.

"You're supposed to say, 'Who's there?'"

Nukilik rolled her eyes. "I know who's there. You're a narwhal."

"No. I'm trying to tell you a joke."

"Well, it isn't funny."

"I haven't gotten to the punch line yet!"

"Just tell me where we are," Nukilik insisted.

"Hold on. I'm trying to break the ice first."

"What ice?"

The narwhal spluttered in frustration, shooting a mist of water from his blowhole. "No. Never mind. Just . . . Let's start over, okay? When I say 'Knock, knock,' you say, 'Who's there?' and then I say, 'Interrupting beluga,' and you're supposed to start in with, 'Interrupting beluga who?' But before you finish, I—"

"That's enough," Nukilik growled. "Either tell me where we are or go away."

"Dude. You just interrupted my interrupting beluga

joke. That's so meta."

Nukilik rose and walked away toward the cave in the rocks where she slept. When would she finally heed Mother's rule about not talking to other species?

"What do I have to do to make a splash around here?" huffed the narwhal, using a flipper to splash water through the slats toward Nukilik. "Why are polar bears always so snooty?" he added, sinking away.

That's a silly question for a predator, coming from its food, Nukilik thought, retreating to her cave.

Later that afternoon, she felt the need to relieve herself, and she went to a particular corner of the enclosure to do her business. Before she was done, she was approached by the strangest animal she had ever seen.

"Your disposal is at my disposal," the bizarre, boxy creature with a metallic sheen droned. Its six legs seemed to consist of wheels. Incredibly, its stomach opened up, and it extended two long arms, one holding a brush and the other a hose, as if it intended to rob her of her pile of used fish.

"Go away!" Nukilik growled at it, incredulous. "I'm busy here!"

"You must surrender your stool." The box with the

open stomach sounded insistent.

Nukilik was firm. "I'm not giving you anything."

"It's your poo-bot," the narwhal called over from the slats. "It demands tribute. It keeps your habitat tidy. There's no point in arguing with it."

Nukilik was now beside herself with indignation. "You go away too!" she commanded. "Now! Or else!"

"Suit yourself." The narwhal sank out of view again.

Nukilik watched in utter disbelief as the strange animal called the poo-bot ate her scat and sprayed down the area afterward. It strolled away, singing a happy series of triumphant beeps.

This place is too unnatural, she thought. *I must find my way home.*

CHAPTER FIVE

NUKILIK

(Ursus maritimus)

The next day, when she came out of the pool, she found a plate of raw fish waiting for her by the rocks. She was incredibly hungry, but she only stared at the meal. It gave off a telltale medicinal scent. If she ate it, she'd wake up strapped to a table while the humans poked her.

She thought about it. Her mind had been racing all day. She was grappling with the possibility that she might never see Mother again. So she ate, and her racing thoughts slowed down. She relaxed into a comfortable crouch and rested her chin on her crossed front paws.

The boom-stick human and her slightly taller male colleague entered the enclosure. Nukilik acknowledged them with an absent huff and let them inspect her. When they spoke to her, she understood their banter.

Wait a minute.

She *understood* them!

"There you go, ya big lug. That's right, sweet thing. Such a fuzz ball, you are."

"Aw, you've been chewing on the fake bone we placed here! That's adorbs. We'll have to get her more."

Why can I suddenly understand your speech? And then she wondered with a chill that raced down her spine: *will you understand me?*

She tried to ask them these questions outright, but her mouth and tongue were too lazy. She fought against sleep.

"She's looking so much better. Let's get her on the gurney and run through the checklist," the woman said.

They rolled her onto a table and then wheeled her back into the cave behind the rocks. They wrapped a tourniquet around her back leg. The male stroked her head and neck, calling her a beautiful creature. Then a large needle came out. Nukilik caught sight of it. The syringe was filled with a clear liquid. A droplet of the serum grew on the silver tip and clung there like a bead.

Nukilik bared her teeth and growled.

The humans backed off a few steps, sharing a concerned glance. They laughed off their nerves. Nukilik felt very heavy. She didn't want to move from her comfortable position. But her eyes were locked on the glistening needle.

"Oh, you don't like the needle?" said the woman affectionately. "A big ol' teddy bear like you? You poor, sweet thing. It's just antibiotics."

The humans shared a look, and they began to approach her again, flanking her on either side. Nukilik turned her head, tracking the needle.

The woman noticed this unexpected behavior and frowned. "Distract her, would you, Felix? She's kind of fixated on what I'm doing."

The man named Felix petted her behind the ears. "Hey, Pooh Bear, look over here at me, will ya? It's okay."

Nukilik ignored him, her eyes locked on the needle. The woman took a step closer.

Nukilik released another low, angry growl. "Don't."

The humans stopped in their tracks.

"Doc, did she just say, 'Don't'?" Felix asked.

Yes, I did, Nukilik thought. But it took too much effort to say more.

The woman called Doc released a small laugh. "Just a weird-sounding growl while she's loopy," she insisted.

Doc and the polar bear locked eyes. Nukilik let her frustration and distrust show. Doc stiffened and fell back a step. Her expression flashed with wonder and then confusion. "Something's not right," she admitted, holding back.

She sees me, Nukilik realized with a flutter of elation. But her eagerness to communicate with the woman suddenly turned to caution. Her mother's warning echoed in her mind: "We don't speak to other species,

Nukilik. Predators must remain above. That is The Way. It's about balance. It's having faith in things we don't comprehend."

Nukilik had little faith in anything anymore. But she would honor her mother's wishes. She looked away from the woman and the needle. With a huge sigh, Nukilik closed her eyes.

She felt a prick on her leg a moment later, and the tourniquet released its tight grasp around her thigh.

The humans guided Nukilik back out into the enclosure and departed through a gate hidden by fake rocks. "So strange," said the woman as they left. "For a moment there I thought she was mad at me."

"Yeah."

"No, I mean, really. Like: she was personally angry. At *me*. I saw it in her eyes. I wouldn't think anything of it, except she's not the first animal around here to give me the stink-eye lately."

"Must be something in the water."

"Don't joke. I'm telling you. Sometimes I feel like these animals are a few steps ahead of me."

"Don't be so hard on yourself," Felix suggested, his

voice drifting away. "We're doing the best we can here, with zero staff."

Nukilik was alone again. She closed her eyes, wishing none of this had happened to her. *I was restored to health, but now I'm trapped here by myself, cut off even from the Old Natures. What purpose is there in that?*

Nukilik vowed to escape the first chance she got.

CHAPTER SIX

NUKILIK

(Ursus maritimus)

After a few days, Nukilik discovered she could move in ways that had once been difficult or impossible. One morning, she lifted a paw, rotated her wrist, and squeezed her digits into a fist. Fascinated, she reached down, picked up a small rock, hefted it in her palm, and threw it across the enclosure, hitting the metal pole she had aimed for.

She sat back, stunned at her own ability, and reached for her chewing bone. "How about that?" she wondered, absently gnawing on it. "What else can I do?" She studied the high walls of her enclosure and visualized ways to escape.

I could pull one of those metal poles from the ground, prop it up on top of the boulders against the wall, and shimmy out. Or I could use it as a lever and pry open the gate. Or easier still: I could fake eating the next meal that smells like medicine and pretend to get sleepy. When the humans enter—I could ambush them and bolt.

"Amazing," she marveled aloud. "The options are endless."

Her body wasn't the only thing that was becoming nimbler. Her mind had grown sharper too.

Are these changes part of growing up? she wondered. *Was Mother hiding this from me?* She laughed at herself. *That can't be it.* Her mother could never throw rocks or imagine such a thing as a lever.

She walked over to one of the metal poles that held up a thick cable running along the top of the pit. She grabbed it with her front paws and began to wiggle it loose.

It felt stiff and firm at first but became easier to wiggle the more she worked at it.

After a moment, a brusque voice startled her out of her task. "Whoa. Um. Hey. Stop that."

Nukilik paused. She looked around for the source of the voice and found a furry orange creature with a big head sitting on top of one of the boulders at the base of her canyon wall. The large animal appeared vaguely similar to humans—but it was definitely not a human. It climbed over the high wall and scrambled down the fake limestone boulders, keeping a healthy distance.

"Greetings," the orange thing said from its safe perch on the boulders.

Nukilik thought hard for a moment, debating whether or not to reply.

"We don't speak to other species."

The polar bear decided to ignore the thing. She gave the metal pole another vigorous shake, bending it.

"Seriously, you're breaking it. I need you to *not* do that. A human will notice."

Nukilik snorted. She didn't turn her head to acknowledge the thing that was trying to order her around, but she did offer an explanation. "Of course I'm breaking it. I'm getting out of here."

"You won't eat me, will you? If I approach?" asked the lanky orange figure sitting on the rock.

The bear stopped shaking the pole again. She thought about it, then offered the creature a sidelong glance. "You're a bit hairy for what little meat you're worth."

The orange fellow raised an eyebrow then rested a palm on his head for a moment. "Fair enough, I suppose." He lowered himself down the rocks and walked using his knuckles along the enclosure floor over to the bear. "I'm Arief. I'm an orangutan."

"I'm Nukilik," answered the polar bear.

"Does your name mean something?"

"One whose nature is strong."

"Ah." Arief nodded, looking the polar bear up and down and glancing at the bent pole. "No one's going to argue with that."

"And what does your name mean?"

"Smart and knowledgeable."

"Ah. Well, if you're so wise, then tell me: where am I?" Nukilik demanded, abandoning the pole for the time being. She sat down. "What is this place? Why am I here? Why are my hands working like a human's? Why can I understand them? And what's an orangutan?"

Arief lowered his head. "Oh, my," he sighed. "You're

full of questions. We should have made first contact sooner. We tried, but . . . I've never seen the narwhal so anxious around a newcomer!"

"The narwhal was annoying," Nukilik grumbled.

The orangutan laughed. "Yes. But Murdock was keeping an eye on you, at my request. There are many animals here at the Ark. I'm a primate, one of only a few types of great apes. The world is a big place, Nukilik, full of creatures you've never imagined."

In spite of Nukilik's hesitation, she found herself liking this ape. He seemed to have answers. "Please," she asked. "What's going on? What's happening to me?"

"You've gone hyper," Arief replied. "Your brain is working more like a human's, and you might even notice some changes in how your body works. It happens to some of the animals here. We don't know how. Or why. The humans don't seem to be aware of our transformation. Which means they're probably not doing it to us. At least not on purpose. But something's at work in this place: once we're here long enough, some of us become more . . ." The orangutan drifted off, struggling for words.

"Like them?" Nukilik tried.

"For better and for worse, yes," Arief confirmed with a sigh.

"Could it be the location itself?" Nukilik wondered. "A natural feature nearby with strange energies?" She thought of the green ribbons in the sky back home, a mysterious quality of the Great Realm that energized all who beheld them.

Arief shook his head. "Can't be. There are plenty of other animals in here—and native ones outside too—who aren't hyper."

"I don't want to be hyper," Nukilik said. "I don't want to think and act the way humans do. What if I forget The Ways? What would I be without my instincts?"

"I know it can be scary and feel like a burden, but I promise you'll learn to live with it."

Nukilik frowned in thought. "Well," she said, "then I'll use it to free myself. I must get back home. My mother is there. She must think that I'm drowned, by now."

What if she *drowned?* Nukilik thought. *I have to make sure that she's okay.* She turned away from the orangutan to hide her expression.

"Answer my question," Nukilik insisted. "Where are

we? Show me the way out."

"What good would that do? We're on an island," Arief said.

Unimpressed, Nukilik waited for more. When it was clear that Arief had explained all he intended to, she grunted. Nukilik had been on and off islands her entire life. Being surrounded by water was no excuse for staying put. Unless . . . maybe this lanky animal couldn't swim? It was a bizarre concept, but some animals could fly and others could not, so maybe it was possible that some creatures simply sank when placed in water.

"I can swim," Nukilik assured him. She looked up, shying her eyes from the day star beyond the glass triangles suspended above. She absently noted that the sun was higher in the sky than she'd ever known it to go, and night and day lasted about the same length of time here. But that was a mystery for later. "If you just show me the dome's exit, I'll be on my way."

A soft, muffled voice cut in on the conversation. Nukilik couldn't make out the words nor exactly where they were coming from. But Arief put a hand to one of his big orange ears, and Nuk realized he had some kind of device clamped to his head.

"Acknowledged. Thanks for the heads-up!" Arief said to the air.

The quiet voice ceased its murmuring, and Arief lowered his hand. "That was Murdock, our narwhal friend, on the radio," he explained to the polar bear.

"How are you speaking to him?" Nuk asked, astonished. "He's not here with us."

"We use radios," Arief explained quickly. "Listen, there's a team of humans visiting today. I need to get back to my jungle hab on the double before they notice I'm missing. Give me a few days, will you? The humans will depart, letting the automated systems run things. I'll swing back through here and answer your questions then. Us hypers: we've formed a team. We call ourselves the Endang—"

"I won't be here in a few days," Nukilik warned. "I'm leaving, with or without your help."

Arief scratched his head. "Nukilik, I don't have time to explain. But you'll put yourself and the rest of us in danger if the humans find out how smart you are. Humans are insatiably curious. The unexplained can make them anxious and desperate—even the nicer ones like Dr. Fellows and Mr. Gooding."

Nukilik remembered her own cautionary instinct the night when she had chosen not to talk to the doctor. A cold chill ran up her back. If she had revealed her ability to speak, there was no telling what might have happened next.

"Please," Arief concluded, "lie low until I can return. There's more at stake here than your own concerns. Our group is secretly making a difference all over the—"

"You don't tell a polar bear what to do." Nukilik narrowed her eyes at Arief. The orangutan might be right to advise caution, but he wasn't in charge of her. "No wonder The Ways frown upon talking to other species. I walk my own path."

Arief sighed. "I'm sorry, I've really gotta go!" The great ape climbed the bent pole and grabbed on to the wire it was hooked to. He swung himself arm after arm across the long cable, over the bear's pool, and up above the far canyon wall, escaping the pit Nukilik was trapped in.

The polar bear watched the strange visitor vanish out of sight, rushing off to some other part of this place he had called the Ark. She straightened the bent pole the best she could and reached for her bone. She growled softly to herself. For now, she might wait—but not for several days.

That orangutan had no right to swing away and expect her to stay put, no matter how dangerous or bizarre the rest of this Ark might be.

CHAPTER SEVEN

ARIEF

(Pongo abelii)

Dangling from the taut cable, Arief hoisted himself up and over the moat of the bear's climate-controlled habitat. He dropped onto a raised concrete walkway known as the skywalk, the floor of which sat just beyond Nukilik's line of sight. The path overlooked a series of enclosures that made up the facility's polar exhibits. From here, he could play tourist, able to peer down at Nukilik's Arctic beach, Murdock's expansive saltwater aquarium, and the still-under-construction Antarctic penguin cove.

These three exhibits represented just a few of the many biomes, or environments, beneath the enormous glass dome. Animals from around the world were being collected here, each living in an artificial habitat built to mimic their real home. The place was known as the Ark, a facility dedicated to protecting the planet's most endangered species.

Arief had been the first animal brought here, but he had been the second to mysteriously acquire humanlike intelligence and dexterity after arriving. The first animal who had gone hyper had tragically died.

Arief pushed those memories away.

After living here for so long, he knew every square inch of the Ark. He'd learned long ago how to move around without being seen.

From his skywalk vantage point, Arief watched an oblong shadowy form rise from the depths of the saltwater tank. Murdock, the friendly neighborhood narwhal, was surfacing. Arief paused, wondering what the excitable whale wanted.

The narwhal's single, arrow-straight tusk breached the surface of the water. Like a mythological unicorn's horn, it stuck straight out in front of his head, extending a

full three feet in length. The tusk was a type of modified tooth, and Murdock used it not as a weapon but to feel out his immediate surroundings by detecting vibrations in the water.

Murdock's face was a mixture of black and white speckles, darker on top and mostly white toward the bottom. He spewed water from his blowhole and craned his beady black eyes up at Arief. "I'm monitoring all video feeds from my command center," he gurgled. "You've got four humans on the doorstep of your hab. If they catch you missing—"

"Wait. The dolphin play corner? You're calling it a command center?" Arief asked.

The narwhal was the Ark's only cetacean so far, but his tank had been built to handle a variety of endangered ocean animals, including dolphins. And deep along one of the aquarium's walls, the humans had installed a full-sensory, subaquatic touch screen computer interface. The equipment had to do with scientists' decades-old desire to figure out how to communicate with dolphins. For some bizarre reason, humans thought dolphins were more intelligent than other creatures. But according to Murdock, humans would be sorely disappointed if they figured out how to communicate, since dolphins only ever wanted to gossip about their friends and relatives. At any rate, Murdock had used the interface to secretly hack into the entire Ark mainframe. He had access to every security camera and every computerized system within, beneath, or above the entire island.

"Don't be a hater. You're wasting time!"

Arief scowled. "I only waited because I saw you rising. Why'd you surface just to yell at me?"

Murdock gurgled, his version of a growl. "Can't a whale breathe every once in a while? Go!"

Arief grunted a protest and knuckle-galloped down the path, stooping to stay hidden behind the walkway's waist-high guard wall. He turned sharply around a corner and locked eyes on his destination: the large glass cube located in the center of the dome, which contained the tropical aviary and the steamy "Jungles of the World" environment.

"A gaggle of four *Homo sapiens* are approaching the cube from the grassland," Murdock reported into Arief's earpiece. "Do you spot them?"

"I've got a visual," the orangutan confirmed.

Men, dressed in suits, crowded the observation post,

looking out upon the home of the Ark's pair of black-footed ferrets. The front entrance to the cube was only a few feet away from them.

"I don't think you can beat them home. You'll have to slip in through the tunnels or backtrack through the desert."

"I'm on the skywalk," Arief reminded him. The Ark's extensive tunnel system offered the animals the best cover for sneaking around, but the nearest stairwell leading belowdecks was behind the aquarium—in the wrong direction. Doubling back would cost precious time he didn't have. "I'll drop right into the desert. Will you see if the ferrets can buy me a few extra seconds?"

"Copy. I'll try Hobbs and Jill, but I don't think their radios are on. Over."

The cube was nearly three stories tall, and it was sealed off from the rest of the dome to keep the air wet and humid inside. It had only two entrances. The doors closer to Arief were located at the edge of the grassland habitat. The other access point was on the far side of the cube, opening into the desert environment. Since the humans were entering the jungle from the grassland, Arief would have to go around or over the cube to reach the more distant desert doors. Then he would have to enter the cube and break back into his own enclosure, all before the visiting humans caught him missing.

He picked up his pace, growing sore and out of breath. He wasn't at his best while knuckle-running for more than a minute at a time—especially along hard concrete—but he couldn't afford for the human visitors to find his enclosure empty. At the very least they would come up with new security procedures that would make it harder for him to move freely about. And at worst, if they realized how smart he was, they might reward him by stabbing a set of electrodes into his open brain—and then everything the hypers here had worked so hard to create would come crashing down.

Arief's heart beat faster and a slight sense of panic started to creep over him. How could he have been so careless? He had spent too much time reasoning with the polar bear. *There's too much at stake for casual errors like that.*

"Our pair of ferrets aren't responding, over," reported Murdock. His voice was only slightly garbled. The subaquatic microphone he used was programmed to filter out most of the gurgling that accompanied underwater talking. "Probably because the humans are lingering in the prairie, checking on them."

"Copy. What about Wan?" Arief asked, huffing his way forward. "Is she back in the cube? She could devise a distraction."

Wangari was an African black-bellied pangolin. She had stayed on the skywalk when Arief entered the Arctic beach enclosure to make first contact with Nukilik. With nimble reflexes and iron-tough armor plates protecting her whole body, Wangari wasn't in danger of being eaten by a polar bear, but there was no point in overwhelming Nukilik with too many new faces all at once.

Murdock spurted a laugh. "She took off after my first warning. She's twice as fast as you. Of course she's home in the cube already."

"Well, tell her to make it rain," Arief directed. "A downpour will fog up the windows on the inside, provide me some cover to climb the outer scaffolding."

"Sounds like a plan, orangutan," agreed the narwhal. Arief could hear him tapping screens with his tusk and his fins. "But she's not on her radio either. I'll bypass the sprinkler system myself. Meanwhile, I'm seeing the humans on the move again. They're entering your hab. Stand by."

Arief stopped where the skywalk came closest to brushing the cube's exterior. From here he could reach out his arms and grip the metal framework then scale down the outside of it. But if he went now, the humans would catch a glimpse of him through the glass. The thought raised the hairs on his neck.

"Orange leader standing by," Arief reported.

A steady afternoon monsoon commenced inside the cube. Not long after, steam began to fog the insides of the windows. "Well done, Murdock," Arief noted under his breath. *Now I can descend without being spotted.*

"You say that like you doubted I might pull it off," quipped the narwhal.

"You're joking, right? Everything's a crapshoot with you."

"Hey, throwing feces is your specialty, monkey brain."

"Call me a monkey again and you'll find out exactly what these opposable thumbs can do," Arief warned as he hopped down the steel bars of the cube. He was much faster when climbing, and he made it to the floor of the desert habitat in no time. He slipped inside the cube's first set of doors and waited for them to shut behind him.

"Entering the back entrance now," he told Murdock. A green light flashed and the second set of doors unlocked. He hastened through them to the cube's open tropical interior. A familiar and comfortable blanket of humidity enveloped him as he darted for cover behind some broad-leafed palms. It was warm in here compared to the chilled polar area.

The four humans had entered the cube through the grasslands entrance and were almost in front of his enclosure. Arief made a stealth dash for the hidden door at the back of his exhibit and ducked inside just in time.

"Made it!" Arief reported.

"Take your headset off, you big ape!" warned Murdock's voice.

"Oh, right, over." Arief flung his earpiece and mic to the ground and kicked them beneath some coiled-up vines.

"He's over here," one of the men called out to the others. The humans gathered around, sheltered from the rain beneath a covered walkway, and pointed through the mesh wiring at Arief. "Hey, Pongo! There you are. Were you hiding? Are you afraid of the storm?"

Arief curled his lips back and offered the team an overly enthusiastic nod. He'd learned that a cartoonish gesture now and then helped to keep humans from catching on to his true intellect. Sure enough, his observers guffawed with delight then made some notes on their clipboards.

Of course, Arief wasn't afraid of the rain at all. He loved the downpours. More than any other aspect of this elaborate jungle habitat, the sound and smell of the rain came closest to reminding him of his childhood rain forest home back in Sumatra.

"The rain shouldn't have come on at this hour," complained one of the others.

"I'll make a note to run a diagnostic on the auto sprinkler," said another. This man was holding a pet carrier, but the mesh gate at the front was turned away from Arief so he couldn't see what was inside. But as the man put the carrier down so he could write himself a note on his clipboard, Arief finally caught a glimpse of the occupant within.

It was their black-footed ferret friend Jill!

Arief stooped forward, casting Jill a worried look. *Where are they taking you?* he hoped his gesture conveyed. As far as he knew, Jill hadn't been scheduled to go off-premises. And she was alone. Her partner, Hobbs, usually went along whenever they were taken from the grassland hab.

Jill must have understood the gist of the orangutan's silent question. She patted her tummy. Her eyes were wide with uncertainty behind their signature bandit mask of dark facial fur. Arief wasn't sure if she was indicating to him that she was feeling sick or hungry or what. He nodded to her discreetly, hoping to express that he'd look into the situation.

Jill gave him a wink in return.

"Do you want an apple, Pongo?" asked one of the men. "We'll get you one tomorrow. We're just making the rounds today, buddy. Dr. Fellows will be by to give you an official checkup in the morning. What do you say?"

Arief stuck out his tongue and sputtered at the strangers, careful not to let his expression betray the actual resentment he felt toward these men. Dr. Caitlyn

Fellows and her assistant Felix Gooding were all right, he supposed. But these suit-wearing baboons were less tolerable than actual baboons—and that was saying something.

The gaggle of humans laughed again and moved off toward the desert exit, checking boxes on their clipboards. They carried Jill away with them.

Arief sat back and listened to the comforting sound of the rain, finally daring to catch his breath.

CHAPTER EIGHT

ARIEF

(Pongo abelii)

"That was a close call."

Arief turned at the sound of the familiar voice coming from the bushes behind him. It belonged to Wangari, the pangolin. She was already out of her enclosure, approaching with her chin raised. "I told you the polar bear would be stubborn."

Arief sighed. "I know. You don't have to make a stink about it."

"Hey, just because I have scent glands—"

"It's only an expression!"

"Fine." Wan eyed him sternly. "Did you get what you wanted? Was it worth the risk?"

"You bet it was."

Wangari ambled out of the ferns and hurried for cover beneath the overhang sheltering Arief. Rain splattered against the beautiful golden-brown scales that made up her natural armor, which whenever she tucked into a ball made her look like a pumpkin-sized artichoke. Wangari had a pointed nose and a freakishly long, sticky tongue curled up inside of her mouth. She walked mostly on her hind legs, like an upright dinosaur, with a lengthy tail trailing out behind her. At only a foot tall, she was stealthy and lightning fast when the occasion called for it—which was getting to be more and more often these days. Wan understood electronics and had a knack for inventing useful spy gadgetry.

Once out of the rain, Wangari quested the ground with her nose, rooting through some fallen leaves. She shot out her tongue and snatched up a quick six-legged snack before parking herself beside Arief. "I'm telling you: that bear is trouble."

The orangutan sighed. "Well, if we weren't there to

stop her, she'd have invented a hang glider by now. The sirens would be blaring, and the whole Ark would be on lockdown. We'd be finished and those men in the suits would be sticking electrodes in our brains."

"You and the electrodes," scoffed Wangari, doing yoga stretches to keep her muscles warm. "You're making my case for me."

"What are you talking about?" Arief asked, pretending to be offended.

"I know you. I know what you're thinking. And I think it's a terrible idea."

Arief snorted. But Wangari was reading him like a book. There was no point in beating around the fig tree. "So, you heard my entire conversation with Nukilik?"

"I caught enough of it. She's a loose cannon. We're going to have to deal with her one way or another."

"She could join us."

Wangari shot the orangutan a disbelieving look. "There it is."

"She'd be quite an asset if—"

"An apex predator? On our team? You're mad. It's out of the question."

Arief let out a wry chuckle. "I don't know. We've

already got a one-ton whale in our ranks. We fought over that decision too, remember? And now he's gotten us access to this place's entire computer network. We've disabled or falsified all their automated monitoring efforts. Who knows what kind of new skills Nukilik could offer? What's the difference if we bring a top predator on board?"

"Um, the number of teeth, for starters!" Wan argued. "And Nukilik's a teenager, Arief. It's plain she thinks she knows everything. I don't like it."

Arief absently picked at his beard hairs. He didn't blame Wangari for her hesitation. She could very well be right, in the end. But Arief's potbellied gut was telling him that Nukilik had potential. He wasn't willing to dismiss the possibilities without further consideration. "She's just worried about her mother," he pointed out. He released a deep sigh. Painful childhood memories about his own mom threatened to flood in, but he held them back. "I can appreciate where she's coming from."

Wangari flicked at a twig beside her, sending a dozen or so surprised ants scattering. They never had a chance. The pangolin's snakelike tongue collected them all up in one sticky sweep. "I can appreciate it too. That's why I say we make Nukilik our next mission. Let's get her back to the Arctic and reunite her with her family ASAP—and be done with her before she gives us away and your noggin becomes a pincushion."

"No." Arief was firm. "Not yet. I want to show her around. See how she reacts. She's trapped here against her will, Wan. Of course she's anxious and acting out. Once she sees that we're actually in charge of the place—once she gets what we're up to . . . she'll come around."

"Why are you putting so much faith in her?" Wangari asked. "You're usually the one who likes to take things slow."

Arief shrugged. "I am taking it slow. I want to see where this goes. You're the one rushing to judgment."

"I'm just calling it how I see it." With a shallow sigh, she surrendered. "We both know the final decision is yours. After you convince Murdock that the idea was his, of course. But I won't hesitate to tell you I told you so when this thing goes sideways."

Arief laughed. "We have time," he insisted. "I convinced Nukilik to wait a few days before doing anything."

"And she was cool with that?"

"Um. Pretty much. I think so. Yes."

"Right."

Arief quickly changed the subject. "The humans had Jill with them. Do you know what that's about?"

"Only Jill?"

"Yeah, Hobbs wasn't with her. She patted her stomach when I tried to ask her what was up. I'm not really sure what she meant."

Wangari gave her own soft underbelly an absent scratch with one of her powerful digging claws. "I heard the humans mention Dr. Fellows as they walked in. I'm sure it's routine. But I'll try and sneak over to the clinic here in a bit."

"That'd be good. Thank you." When humans were on the island, it was harder for Arief to sneak around in the Administrative wing. Wan was the team's go-to ninja in such instances.

The rain shut off with the abruptness of a flipped switch. The tropical birds in the trees sang their appreciation for the change in weather and began flitting about. Arief heard another noise in the rain's sudden absence. He couldn't place it.

He panned his ears across the forest floor, trying to

figure out what he was hearing. It sounded like a voice, but an impossibly small one. *Great clouded leopard,* he thought, still scanning the ground. *Are the insects talking now?* His mind raced with the possibility that the Ark might be transforming a non-mammal species into a hyper. *A smart bug? Our first hyperintelligent non-mammal! I'll have to convince Wan not to eat it!* But his wonderment only lasted a second, until he caught a familiar inflection in the high-pitched voice.

"Arief! Come in, over!"

"Oh, it's Murdock," the orangutan grumbled, remembering how he had swept his headset into the jungle understory a few moments ago. He fished through the coiled vines and rotting leaves at the base of the strangler fig and found his earpiece. The narwhal sounded frantic. Arief hurriedly shook the mud from the radio and put the audio bud in his ear. "I'm reading you, Murdock. Go ahead."

"We have a code blue!" gurgled the whale. "I repeat! A code blue!"

"What's a code blue?" asked Arief, sharing a puzzled look with Wangari, who also shrugged. He was pretty sure they hadn't developed a system of codes yet.

"Just get back over here, *stat*!" Murdock sputtered. "Nukilik broke out of her hab. She's heading for the exits."

"What? No!" Arief felt a stab of disappointment before the panic set in. Wangari had been right, after all.

Arief braced himself. "Nukilik's out," he admitted to the pangolin.

"I told you so," Wan said flatly. But she didn't gloat for long. "So, what do we do now?"

"Told him so, what?" asked a new voice, startling both of them.

It was Nukilik! She sat on the path under the covered walkway, her forearms folded as she stared suspiciously at the pair through the mesh wiring of the orangutan enclosure.

Arief barked a laugh of relief that echoed to the canopy, sending birds scattering. He wasn't surprised she had found his hab. Her nose, after all, was one of the biggest sniffers he'd ever seen. "Nothing," he answered the polar bear. "Forget it. I'm just glad to see you here and not, well, running off. But since you're clearly not going to stay put, we might as well show you around."

"Don't try anything," Nukilik cautioned. "I'm not in the mood for any tricks."

"I will never disrespect you, Nukilik," Arief promised.

"I might, if you disrespect us!" the pangolin warned. "I'm not as wise or patient as this old ape. But if you behave, I'll behave. Deal?"

Nukilik placed a bone in her mouth and offered them a wry smile. "I'm still trying to figure out what in the great green ribbons you are. Closest I can figure is some kind of crustacean? Maybe a giant land krill?"

Wangari gasped. "I'm a *pangolin.*"

"She's a type of flightless, toothless pigmy dragon," Arief teased.

"Very funny, big guy," she said sarcastically. She turned back to Nukilik. "I'm a mammal just like you are."

Nukilik didn't look convinced, but she seemed to let her guard down a bit. "Call me Nuk," she told them.

"I'm Wangari. Wan, if you like," replied the pangolin.

"Nuk, come on. Let's go for a walk," said Arief.

"Okay. I am a bit curious about this place," the polar bear said. "But I make no promises to stay here."

Arief couldn't hide a smile. Nukilik was giving them

a chance! It was, perhaps, all they could ask for from a moody apex predator who'd never left the far north before. But this was good. Maybe his dream of a new-fangled team of wildlife defenders would grow by one today, after all.

The orangutan turned and looked down at the astonished pangolin, catching her eye. It was his turn to tell Wan, "I told you so." But he didn't. He took the high road and simply nodded instead.

CHAPTER NINE

NUKILIK

(Ursus maritimus)

Nukilik waited on the covered path as the orangutan and the strange land crab made for the secret exit of Arief's enclosure.

The central path was surrounded on all sides by tall lush trees and dense plant life. The walkway railings glistened with dew droplets in the thick jungle air, and the path included a metal bridge over a meandering stream fed by a noisy waterfall. It was strikingly more humid in here than anywhere else she'd been within the Ark. Nuk found it curious how this habitat was walled off from the dome, contained within a large cube made of giant windowpanes. A prison within a prison.

A colorful bird swooped low over the path, chirping and disappearing into the bushes. Nukilik tracked its sudden movement and noticed Wangari and Arief standing near the upstream entrance. The strange devices they used to communicate remotely were draped from their necks like jewelry.

"This place was made to approximate your home?" she asked the pair.

"It's called a jungle." Wangari beamed. "Very different from the Arctic. There are many different kinds of jungles, rain forests, and cloud forests throughout the world. The forests where pangolins come from in Africa are pretty different from the ones where orangutans live in southeast Asia, but this gives you a feel for both, I guess. Arief and I are the only hypers in this hab, but there's also lots of birds and frogs and insects and fish in here too. And others will be put here, eventually, once this place becomes fully inhabited by at-risk wildlife. My fenced area is right over there," Wangari pointed out.

"Let's talk as we go," Arief suggested. "I want to stop in the grassland and check on Hobbs. Our ferret friends are hypers, but Hobbs and Jill were just separated from each other and we don't know why."

They set off into the antechamber exiting the cube. A large bird—astonishingly, far more colorful than a puffin—tried to leave with them, but the outer doors would not open.

"Get back in there, macaw!" Arief waved the flapping bird away, and it retreated into the trees, speaking loudly in an animal language that Nukilik had never heard before. Finally, the inner door closed and the outer set of doors opened, allowing them to exit the cube. "Could you understand that bird?" Nukilik asked her guides.

"Yes," Wangari said. "But only just barely. The New World tropical dialects are pretty unique to their region. He was looking for the beach. He hasn't gone hyper, though, so he doesn't really understand what the deal is around here."

"What *is* the deal around here?" Nukilik asked.

They stepped together into the grassland. Nuk noted the immediate drop in humidity with a sense of relief.

Arief took a breath. "This place is called the Ark. It's kind of a safe zone, where we can live without facing the threats of the outside world."

"The humans think we want this?" Nukilik asked incredulously.

Arief shook his head. "No. I don't think they do. But they don't know what else to do either. Some of them understand they've destroyed our world. They want to help, but they don't know how. Most animals brought here are at risk or endangered."

"Endangered?" Nukilik asked. "What does that mean?"

The orangutan rubbed his chin. "You see, all of us here . . . we belong to different species that aren't doing well in the wild anymore. Wan, for example, was rescued from the bottom of a crate at an airport. She was being smuggled from her home in Africa to be made into soup for humans to eat. She was nearly dead when she was found, and she was sent here for safekeeping. The humans who run this place . . . they've collected us in order to protect us."

Nukilik considered this for a long moment. She remembered back to her final days in her Realm. She and Mamma had been starving to death. Neither of them had seen another polar bear for too long, which was not normal.

The polar bear removed the bone she had been gnawing. Finally, she said, "Endangered. I understand. Yes, these humans saved me. But it was also humans who separated me from my mother."

With a sigh, Nukilik popped the bone back into her mouth and looked around. The pathway the animals were walking down was separated from the grassland habitat's wildlife enclosures by a wire mesh fence. The grassy landscape beyond was peppered with holes and hardened mounds of dirt. A creature raised its slender head from one of the burrows and bounded over to them. It stopped at the fencing and stood on its hind legs, gripping the wire net in its front paws.

"Guys!" the thing said excitedly. It was a bit smaller than the pangolin, and it was covered in fur instead of hard plates. Its arch-shaped body was tan, but its triangular face was paler, with eyes ringed in black. Nukilik was familiar with the likes of this species. She'd seen polar stoats back in the Great Realm, though they were always quick and sly and she'd never seen one up close.

"Hobbs, hi," said Arief. "We saw they took Jill. Is she okay?"

"They're doing some tests on her."

"Did you hear them say why?"

"Yes! They think she's pregnant!"

"Wow! Congratulations, Hobbs," offered Wangari when no one else spoke up. "We were afraid it was something bad."

"It's great," Hobbs said. "Our species can use every healthy litter we can get."

"Can I introduce you to Nukilik?" said Arief. "We're showing her around."

"I saw her bounding through here a few minutes ago," Hobbs said. He offered Nuk a friendly wave through the fencing. "You're a kind of bear, right?"

"The mightiest and the proudest," Nukilik answered.

"No arguing that!" Hobbs agreed.

A shrill yip pierced the quiet. Nukilik looked around for the source but found nothing.

"The prairie dogs are lying low right now because I'm out," Hobbs explained.

Nukilik did a double take, thinking of wolves or foxes. "There are dogs here?"

"Oh. No. They're not dogs. They're actually rodents. You know, mice and rats and squirrels and chipmunks and beavers . . . Prairie dogs are members of the squirrel family of rodents, except they live underground and not in trees. Black-tailed prairie dogs and Gunnison's prairie dogs are a ferret's main sources of food."

This ferret seems to be glad that he's here, Nuk told herself. *Protected. But his kits are going to grow up soft and lazy, hunting caged food. And then what?*

She huffed and rotated the bone in her mouth, stewing. *I would never have cubs here. They'd be good for nothing in the wild.*

"Is Nukilik thinking of joining the team?" Hobbs asked.

Nukilik stared at him.

"Well, we'd better hurry along," Wangari said quickly. "We really don't have much time."

"What team?" Nukilik demanded. "I warned you: no tricks."

"There's nothing sneaky going on, Nuk," Arief said. "We work as a group. If you're interested in joining us, I'll tell you more."

"I'm not." The polar bear snorted in reply. "Polar bears don't do teams. Especially not with other species."

They said goodbye to the ferret and led Nukilik

behind a stairwell entrance disguised as a granite boulder. A strong wind blew when Arief opened the door. The sounds of loud generators and pumps echoed up from the darkness. They descended a short flight of metal stairs.

"An interconnected maintenance tunnel system runs under the Ark," Arief explained, pressing forward into the breezy, darkened corridor. "We use the humans' own monitoring systems against them—sensors hidden everywhere warn us when people are moving about. Then we track them with the cameras. Meanwhile, they just get fed videos of us on our best behavior, in a loop."

Wan added, "This place is mostly automated. It's designed to have a bare minimum of humans on-site, so the inhabitants never become accustomed to people. Right now, they're expanding and constructing new habs, so it's busy. But believe me, we've vanished for days at a time before, no problem."

"They want us to be able to survive here, long term, in the event that something catastrophic occurs among their kind," Arief added.

They quietly weaved through the corridors,

navigating complex machinery and plumbing and tubes and cylindrical vats filtering salt water and fresh water.

The gate swung open and they passed out of the windy maintenance tunnel onto a dune of fine black sand. They had entered another habitat. An uneven black slab lay on the ground between the dune and the lapping water of another pool. "Welcome to the Hawaiian Island exhibit. That's lava rock." Arief pointed. "There are coral formations in the pool. Try not to break them; it'll make the humans suspicious because this exhibit doesn't have a 'main attraction' endangered animal yet, just some colorful fish."

"And the moray eel," Wangari intoned. "My advice: stay away from the dark nook over where there's a gap in the coral."

Arief frowned at Wangari. "The moray eel won't hurt you, Wan. She might look scary with her sharp teeth, but they have terrible eyesight and eat only small fish."

"Whatever you say. I always try to keep an eye out for things with big sharp teeth," Wangari replied, glancing pointedly at Nuk.

They made their way into the water, which was

unpleasantly warm for Nuk's taste. The reef beneath them was colorful, gleaming red and yellow here and there, with seaweed and other aquatic plants swaying to the rhythm of the current. As they swam, the water grew cooler.

"We are approaching the gate," Arief chanted, speaking into his microphone while paddling. Nukilik heard a tinny Murdock reply, "Copy that," and the metal grates in the pool's downstream divider slid into the wall. They each dove through the opening and surfaced in a new enclosure similar in size to Nukilik's Arctic beach.

They pulled up on shore and shook themselves dry.

"This is the penguin habitat," Arief said.

Nukilik glanced sidelong at Wangari. "More pangolins here?"

"*Penguins*, not pangolins. Very different," Wangari corrected. "This hab isn't finished, so be careful of humans doing construction work and making unscheduled appearances. We should be good for now because everyone's at lunch."

"What are penguins?" Nuk asked.

"South Pole birds," Arief explained. "Nothing you'd know of up north. They don't fly, though, except through the water. There's a pair of northern rockhopper penguins, and their chick." He pointed. "Status: endangered, with populations decreasing."

Nukilik followed the orangutan's gesture and saw two upright, black-and-white creatures with wavy yellow eyebrows cuddling a fledgling chick. They were nestled into a hollow of fake rock with an unfinished side. A metal framework poked through the fake rock face. Above the birds was a scaffolding littered with construction tools. Nuk noticed a sleeping poo-bot parked in a nook in the unfinished rock wall.

"Careful," Murdock warned loudly through the others' headsets so Nukilik could hear him. "They like to argue. They insist that *they're* from the top of the world, and that the Arctic is at the bottom."

"Why are they here if the habitat isn't done?"

"Sometimes rescue animals are brought to Dr. Fellows, and she doesn't turn them away. Next door is your enclosure, Nukilik."

Nukilik wouldn't have believed the animals were birds if it weren't for the hatchling's obvious juvenile feathers.

More babies growing up caged, she thought. Something

about that idea terrified her. And something else about what she was looking at punched her in the gut. It only took her a moment to identify the source of her uneasiness.

At least that fledgling has its mother.

Heartsick, Nukilik *gnarred* involuntarily. Arief and Wangari watched her cautiously.

She grunted. It turned to a growl and then an outright snarl of anger. "I'm sorry," she told them. "This isn't working. I don't want to be here. I don't want to be hyperintelligent. I'm leaving. Don't try to stop me."

One of the penguins said something. It was accompanied by what appeared to be an angry hush and a gesture toward the napping chick between its legs. But Nukilik didn't know the language it used. How could there be so much in the world that she didn't know, that The Ways had never prepared her for?

She slammed forward on all fours with a thud that made the ground quake. Nukilik bounded past the penguin family and leaped up onto the structure of unfinished rocks, scanning for a way out. She saw it: a low point in the incomplete wall that she could reach by climbing the scaffolding.

"Nukilik!" cried Wangari. "Listen! There's nowhere for you to go!"

"Let her go, Wan." Arief sighed. "We tried, but it's clear she needs to find out the truth about this place in her own way."

Nukilik didn't wait to hear any more. She scrambled onto the scaffolding and over the wall.

CHAPTER TEN

WANGARI

(Phataginus tetradactyla)

Wangari watched as Nukilik leaped onto the scaffolding, which wobbled dangerously under her weight. The polar bear clambered onto the skywalk and disappeared from view. Wangari winced. For a moment the scaffolding looked like it might tip and crash, but it finally stopped swaying.

"We can't just let her loose," Wangari protested to the great ape beside her. "Let's show her what we're made of."

"We could do that," Arief said, "but we're not going to. She doesn't trust us. Laying her flat with your signature leg sweep will only humiliate her and make things worse."

"It's a tail sweep, in my case. And it just might humble her a bit."

"Yes. And then she'll eat you. Let her go. She needs to see the truth for herself."

"But what if she's spotted?" Wangari barked angrily. "What if she barrels down the Admin hall?"

Arief rubbed his chin. "Let's clear her a path," he said. "It's the best we can hope for."

"On it." Wangari scrambled up the rock formations. At the top, she flipped as a tight ball onto the scaffolding, uncurling just in time to plant her feet on the platform. Lashing out her tongue like a whip, she wrapped it around an iron bar above her, and launched herself forward. She built momentum, swinging higher and higher, and finally let go at the peak of her arch. Her body sailed through the air and she touched down on the skywalk in a gentle crouch.

"Turn on your radio!" Arief called up to her.

Wangari lifted the headset dangling around her neck and pressed the buds into her ears. "I'm receiving, over."

"Do you *mind*?" one of the rockhopper penguins

squawk-whispered from the ground. "You clearly have *no* idea how hard it is to keep a baby asleep. Winter's around the corner, and we need our rest."

"Sorry," Wangari offered—too loudly, by the looks it got her.

Nukilik, up ahead along the high path, paused, staring thoughtfully down at her own enclosure. Wangari hurried toward the polar bear, silent as the wind.

But Nukilik saw movement and recognized Wangari. She fled toward a stairway at the end of the skywalk.

"Polar bear's loose again! Looks like she's on a real rampage this time," Murdock warned them over the radio.

"We know," answered Arief's voice. "Wangari is in pursuit."

The gate to the stairwell swung automatically shut before Nukilik reached it.

"That oughta stop her!" trumpeted the narwhal.

Wangari approached the cornered polar bear cautiously.

Nukilik bared her teeth at the pangolin. "You can't keep me here."

Wangari took a deep breath. "I'm not trying to."

Nukilik leaped from the raised pathway.

Wangari gasped. She flipped onto the narrow railing to watch as the polar bear plunged. Nukilik crashed into the marine aquarium fifty feet below, causing a thunderous splash.

"What in the Northwest Passage was *that*?" Murdock sputtered. "I just felt an explo— Wait a minute. *That crazy bear's in the tank with me!*"

Wangari glared down. Nukilik was visible as a blurry blotch swimming beneath the water. The polar bear's head breached the surface, and she glanced around, registering a way out of the pool. Nuk shot for the exit with a powerful paddle stroke.

Wangari's armored plates stood on end. "She's heading for the petting pad." It was designed to allow humans to lean out over the pool and observe the sea mammals. The polar bear could scramble over the splash guard from there, no problem.

The orangutan sounded out of breath through the headset. "Try and redirect her toward the desert. I'm heading there now. There's the outer exit past the cacti—far from crew activity. Over."

"Copy." The pangolin raced along the narrow rail but

realized she wouldn't reach Nukilik in time, unless . . .

She eyed an iron crossbeam angled between two concrete columns that extended down to the petting platform. "That'll do," she told herself with a smile. She launched off the railing, her forearms extended. Her tongue lashed out and gripped the crossbeam. As it snapped tight, she was flung forward. Her long, curved claws caught the crossbeam's edge, letting her zip-line down the steel beam in one long effortless move. Then, right before she slammed into the column, Wangari swung hard to one side and tucked into a ball, rolling along the aquarium's concrete edge. Nukilik was just climbing onto dry ground beside the observation lean-out when Wangari skidded to a halt in front of her.

"Humans are crowding the conference room," Murdock reported.

Wangari sidled over, physically blocking the path leading to the Admin hall. The polar bear shook herself dry and glowered at the pangolin.

"The humans are corralled back this way, Nuk," Wangari pleaded, her arms extended. Her voice was small and nervous. She cleared her throat and tried again. "You can't—"

"Stop telling me what I can't do," Nuk interrupted, somewhat surprised at Wan's sudden appearance. "Out of my way!" The polar bear lifted a front paw angrily—and swatted at the pangolin.

Wangari's eyes shot wide open. She tucked into a plated ball, bracing for the blow. It came, hard and swift. She was suddenly airborne, like a soccer ball kicked from midfield toward the goal. She bounced, tumbled, then unraveled. Her paws gripped the concrete floor and she braked with her tail.

The pangolin and the polar bear locked eyes. For a terrifying moment, Wangari thought Nukilik would rush at her. *I might as well stop a train.* But Wan rose as tall as she could, puffed her plates, and opened her arms.

"Don't go . . . this way!"

"What's really over there?" Nuk demanded. "The easiest way out?"

The pangolin's patience snapped. Wangari sprinted toward the polar bear. Nukilik backed off a step, her expression more amused than fearful. Wangari took full advantage of the polar bear's uncertainty. She leaped. She spun. She landed—right on Nukilik's shoulder. She thrust a well-placed claw into the polar bear's neck,

crushing the nerve core she knew would be there, and sent the white giant into convulsions.

Nukilik roared in pain and collapsed, hammering the ground with her enormous paws. Wangari dismounted and landed upright next to her.

"Ow!"

"We're not against you, Nukilik. We're your friends." Wangari growled, looking square into the polar bear's stunned eyes while standing over her. "We could have taken you down anytime. We're your equals. Now grow up."

Nukilik glared at her. But then her eyes softened. "I'm not looking for friends. I'm looking for my family." She stood up, chose another route, and bounded away, escaping Wangari's view.

"Nuk's headed for the desert now," she advised with an explosive sigh, and took off after the polar bear at a pangolin sprint.

Hobbs chimed in through the radio, breathing fast. "I'll meet you and Arief there." The ferret had apparently turned on his headset at some point. "Sorry I'm late to the party. But we need to disarm the emergency exits before Nuk leaves."

Over at the desert, the white polar bear was obvious, pushing through a patch of light green paloverde trees as she searched off-path for a new direction. The facility walking paths dead-ended at the desert, marked by the steep outer wall of the dome as it rose from the floor skyward, arching far overhead. The surface of the exterior dome was made of a thin cloudy plexiglass that obscured Wangari's view of the outside world beyond.

With her armored body, Wan had no problem marching past the cacti. But the polar bear was running into problems. Prickly pears and chollas peppered the terrain, and Nukilik grunted and growled as she shouldered through them, looking for a way out.

"I can't override the alarm," Murdock announced. "Not without shutting down other systems that'll create suspicion."

"Don't worry about it," reported Hobbs. "I'll disarm it manually."

Wangari stole a glance over at the emergency hatch partially hidden behind the grove of paloverde trees. Hobbs was there, clinging to the exit's ovular frame, inspecting the electrical box beside the hatch.

"Nukilik!" Wangari called out, hoping to distract

the polar bear and buy the ferret a few more precious moments to complete his task.

"What's wrong with these horrible bushes!" the bear snarled, flicking away cholla buds, only to have more of them needle into her as she thrashed this way and that. "Why are they attacking me?"

"Come back to the path," Wangari urged.

"Nukilik, I'm sorry."

Wangari turned, startled. It was Arief, who had finished clambering down the skywalk's support column behind the pangolin, leaning on his fore-knuckles, still panting after his mad dash from the penguin habitat. She studied his pained expression. The orangutan's eyes bore a deep empathy, hinting at something of the painful past Wan knew he guarded.

The polar bear stopped struggling in the cholla patch. A quiet settled over the desert.

"The exit is right there." Arief pointed. "Through the trees. It's all yours. We'll be here if you need us."

Hobbs yanked a wire out of the control panel beside the hatch. He hopped to the floor and called over. "Figured it out. The alarm's disengaged."

Nukilik went to the exit at the base of the dome and gave the wheel lock a spin. The hatch swung open. Balmy air carrying a hint of salt rushed to Wan's snout. The polar bear, seeming surprised by her sudden success, lifted her nose to sniff the breeze, and disappeared outside.

CHAPTER ELEVEN

NUKILIK

(Ursus maritimus)

Finally, I'm out!

Nukilik galloped away from the dome. She intended to flee first, think later. *I just need a little distance, then I'll make a plan.*

A short way off, hidden from view behind a low hill and a wall of trees, she could hear waves rushing up against a shore and sea foam crackling as it soaked into sand. Birds were calling, and she could taste a salty punch to the air. All of this was familiar enough. But the air here was warm, and the sun was nearly straight overhead.

No snow. No ice.

She headed for the trees, desperate to learn what lay beyond. On the other side she found a reddish sandy beach peppered with big black rocks. An array of brown boulders blocked her path forward. A white bird with bright blue feet waddled along the shore.

The horizon was a distant, razor-sharp blue-on-blue.

No way I can swim that far.

Arief had warned her they were on an island, but . . . "No." She pressed forward, placing her front paws on top of the closest boulder.

I'll swim for weeks—months!—if I have to. I will *find my way back to where the sun isn't so high and the birds know my name.*

The boulder beneath her moved. Nukilik hopped back, startled. Four scaly fat legs and a head at the end of a long neck emerged from the rock's underbelly.

The giant rock creature lifted its head to study Nukilik.

"What are you?" Nukilik asked it.

The rock thing said something in its own tongue,

slowly, that Nukilik had no hope of translating. She saw deep wisdom in its eyes but no hyperintelligence. This relieved her for some reason. *We're not all lost to this madness*, she thought.

"I'm sorry. I can't understand you," she told the creature.

Maybe a mainland shore would be visible from elsewhere. She needed to see more of the island.

Nukilik gave the strange creature a nod and doubled back through the line of trees, taking in her first full glimpse of the facility she'd escaped. The Ark's dome was enormous. Its outline, defined by the triangular steel framework, curved into a perfect half sphere, flattening slightly at the very top.

She studied the half bubble's summit, realizing it would provide her the perfect view of the island in all directions. *Can I climb it?* she wondered. The slope looked manageable, if the glass wasn't too smooth against the pads of her paws and if the panes were thick enough to hold her weight.

She decided to give it a try.

Along the way, she noticed Arief watching her from the open hatch to the desert, a gusty breeze flowing into the dome that rustled his shaggy hair. He waited there as Nukilik passed by, staying quiet, probably hoping the bear would start a conversation.

Nukilik ignored him.

Instead, she tried her weight on the first triangular pane rising out of the ground. It felt very solid. Her paws achieved good traction. She hoisted herself up, planting all four feet on the glass. She waited there for a moment, testing out just how sturdy she was, and then pressed higher and higher, one paw at a time, until her feet were steady beneath her and she could ascend with confidence. Every next pane was at a gentler angle, and her climb grew easier. When she had almost reached the halfway point, she glanced down and noticed Arief effortlessly climbing after her from a short distance away.

Finally, panting, the bear reached the edge of the leveled-off summit, where she had ample space to roam in a circle and study the whole island. After again testing her weight on the glass panes—the ground beneath looked so far below!—she stood on her hind legs and slowly turned 360 degrees.

The island was small. She could probably walk the entire coast in a day. But the terrain was different everywhere, with steep conical hills to the west, gentler forested slopes to the east and the north, and green valleys skirted with beaches to the south. All around, blue bays were ribbed with sea waves.

Other, smaller islands were nearby, covered with jungle and sand. But everywhere in the distance, in all directions, the horizon was a solid line of ocean meeting sky.

"No," she said in a hoarse whisper. She sat down. Her eyes stung, and she blinked away tears.

Arief took a seat beside her. "Did you notice the giant tortoises?" he asked.

"The big rock animals? Yes."

"Some of them are nearly one hundred years old. They're worth getting to know."

"They speak very slowly," Nukilik complained. "And I don't know their words."

"That's because we're half a world away from your home, Nukilik. The humans call these islands the Galápagos. Here the sun rises and sets every day of the year, and the days are almost all the same length, no matter the season."

That's not possible, Nukilik thought. In the Great Realm, entire months of the year passed with the sun barely peeking above the horizon. How could the sun act so differently here? Why did the tortoises and macaws and penguins all speak in gibberish to her untrained ears? But Nuk had seen enough strange things today to convince her that there was much about the world she didn't know. Like that pangolin, for example. *That little lobster took me down!* she marveled. *What else will keep surprising me?*

Nukilik released a deep sigh.

Arief patted the polar bear on the shoulder. "I know why you needed to see for yourself."

"What am I supposed to do?" Nukilik asked him.

"You have us. We can get you home, Nuk. Or you can join us." He plucked a cholla bud from the polar bear's fur and flicked it away. They watched it bounce down the glass dome, gathering speed as it tumbled.

Nukilik studied the orangutan. "How would you help me?"

Right then a startling *thunk!* came from the glass panel beside them. A black circle had appeared underneath it. Nukilik looked hard through the glass and saw a wire dangling from the circle. As she peered down, following the cable to its dizzying end far below, she saw what was attached to it.

Wangari.

The wire grew shorter and shorter, disappearing into a large device strapped to the pangolin's back, carrying her to the ceiling until she was right below them on the other side of the glass. She stabilized herself with a second suction cup.

Smiling up at Nuk and Arief, she drew a rod with a sharp diamond edge from the harness she wore. She used it to score a circular hole out of the glass panel. She slid the cutout away and climbed up through the hole.

"Hi, gang!"

"That was unnecessarily risky," Arief complained. "It's bad enough that *we're* up here."

"I've been meaning to practice with the suction cup launcher." Wangari fit the glass circle back into the windowpane and used some type of goo to seal it in place. She took a moment to arrange all the tools on her harness and then sat down next to them, taking in the view.

"So, where are we in the conversation?" she asked.

“The sensitive part,” griped Arief. “Thanks for interrupting.”

“Excellent. I made it in time for the good stuff. Don’t mind me. Continue.”

Nukilik grunted, then told Wangari, “You’re smart. You’re strong. And now I see that you’re also crazy. Where I’m from, we keep a close eye on types like you.”

“Thank you. Try to keep it in mind next time you treat me like a soccer ball.”

The polar bear hung her head.

Wan gave her a wink. “You’re not the only one of us to freak out when we first go hyper. You’re just the biggest.”

Arief and Wangari both laughed without explanation. Wangari held a claw to her earpiece while smiling, then she answered a comment that Nukilik hadn’t heard. “You’re right, Murdock. You might be four times heavier, but you’re hardly intimidating out of the water.”

Nukilik detected angry shouting after that. Wangari and Arief removed their headsets and held them away at a safe distance.

"I feel left out," Nukilik said. "When do I get one of those?"

Arief arched an eyebrow. "Do you want one?"

Nukilik realized she had backed herself into a trap. She scolded herself with a low growl.

"I'll make you one," Wangari insisted. "We stole a whole box of radios a while back. I gut them for parts then use the 3D printer to design new casings that fit on our different noggins. It's a cinch."

Nukilik heaved a sigh. "Why all the equipment and the teamwork and the advanced fighting techniques?"

"We call ourselves the Endangereds," Arief declared, a glint of pride in his eyes. "We help wildlife across the globe, especially any species red-listed as threatened or endangered. Getting you home and reunited with your mother could be our next mission, Nukilik. But I'd rather recruit you to be our newest team member."

Something Nukilik's mother had said just before they separated suddenly rang in her head. *"You were made with a great purpose in mind."*

To be a part of a team that helped other animals . . . that sounded purposeful. But what would she be sacrificing?

Her home.

Her mamma.

Her natural self.

Nukilik looked down past her lap through the glass. Every environment down there was *fake.* Could she make this place her home?

No.

The Ark could never replace the Great Realm.

But more important, she didn't want to stay like the humans.

"This hyperintelligence that we have: is it . . . permanent?"

"I don't know," Arief confessed. He stroked the hairs beneath his chin for a moment. "Only one hyper has been away from the Ark long enough to answer that question. He died in the wild before I could find out."

"What happened?" Nukilik asked.

Arief took a moment to gather his thoughts. "He was a friend. A quokka, a type of wallaby, native to the small islands off the coast of Western Australia."

"I didn't understand any of that," Nukilik admitted.

"Sorry. Just think of him as a kangaroo about the

size of a house cat who only lives in a very small area on the other side of the globe."

"That still doesn't do me much good," grumbled the polar bear. "But I'll catch on."

Arief rubbed his head and started over. "I was the first animal brought here, but the quokka showed up soon afterward. He went hyper before I did." Arief smiled, looking wistful. "The humans called him Willie the Wallaby, which he hated, but the name stuck. The smarter he got, the more resentful he became. Willie was the one who helped me hijack the aircraft we use." Arief chuckled, but his mind was still far off.

Wangari laughed too. "I wasn't around yet, but I know the story. It's a funny one. But that's for another time."

"Anyway," continued Arief, "we dreamed up the Endangereds together, but he didn't live long enough to see the group come to life. He was selected for reintroduction back into the 'wild.' Willie was excited to settle into a new permanent home. He was shipped off to a 'safari-themed' wildlife park somewhere in California."

"We might as well drop you off in the African

Serengeti, Nukilik," Wangari explained, shaking her head. "Let you make a go of it there."

Arief pressed on. "I heard from him once after he arrived. And then a couple months later I overheard one of the suits talking to Dr. Fellows about how Willie's resettlement 'didn't take.' That's how he described it. Willie the Wallaby, my friend, died ten thousand miles from his natural home, and the guy in the fancy suit only said the effort 'didn't take.'"

All three animals sat in silence for a while, with nothing but the salty breeze and the distant rustling of waves and the occasional calls of unfamiliar birds rising to Nukilik's ears.

"How did Willie die?" Nukilik asked.

"I'm not sure," said Arief, gritting his teeth. "I hacked into the records, but all I found was a reference to 'predation from above.' I think that means he was hunted by a hawk, or something along those lines."

Nukilik had a thousand questions. But none of them mattered. "I'm very sorry to hear about your friend." She heaved a loud sigh. "I understand why he resented this place. I'm sorry, but I can't join your team, Arief."

"Oh?" probed the great ape. "Are you sure you don't want more time to decide? Things have moved very quickly this morning."

Nukilik did feel sure, though she also struggled with a sense of regret at the same time.

"You were made with a great purpose in mind."

Her mother might be right, but it was the memory of her voice—not her words—that spoke to Nukilik loudest of all now.

She nodded. "I just want to go home. I need to find my mother."

Arief scratched his head. Nuk could tell he was disappointed. But he didn't argue back. "I will respect your decision. We have our next mission: we'll get you home."

Wan tsked. "The folks around here will have fits when their new polar bear vanishes."

Arief sighed. "It'll be a mystery, but our responsibility is to our fellow animals, not to those who think they run this place."

Wangari cleared her throat. "Well," she began slowly, "ID'ing your specific home may be difficult."

"I know what it looks like. There's a very distinctive cliff that comes out beyond the water and cuts the beach in two. Big ships visit the area."

"That probably narrows our search parameters down to an area about the size of Pluto," Wangari quipped.

"The Arctic's a big place," Arief pointed out. "We're not going to have the fuel or the time to comb every last inch of it before you recognize where we ought to land."

"I'll get you on the computers in the evenings," Wangari assured her. "The internet database should have plenty of geotagged photos. Eventually you'll recognize something, and we'll triangulate that with other data points and then make a plan to get you back."

"I have no idea what you're talking about," Nukilik grumbled impatiently.

"You'll learn," said Arief. "Meanwhile, during your stay—you're family."

"I'll do my best," said Nukilik grudgingly, "to make the most of the time I have here."

CHAPTER TWELVE

NUKILIK

(Ursus maritimus)

"Nukilik? You awake?"

The polar bear felt a gentle nudge to her side and followed the voice back to wakefulness. "Wan?"

"I'm here to escort you to headquarters."

Nukilik sat up and rubbed her eyes. She was back in her Arctic beach hab. The enclosure was moonlit. Running lights along the visitor path above the moat provided faint additional lighting. Otherwise, the Ark was dim.

"Are you ready to start your computer search tonight?" Wangari asked.

Nuk found a new bone on the ground and clamped it between her teeth. "I've been thinking: would information about my extraction point be with Dr. Fellows?"

"That's good!" praised the pangolin. "The problem is, we already reviewed your file when you arrived. Standard procedure—just in case newbies go hyper. We couldn't access your collection point data from here."

"But why?"

"Humans deal a lot with something they call 'red tape.' It may take months before your paperwork is digitized. And the hard copy isn't on the island. Short of directly asking Fellows where she found you, our options for pinpointing your home are limited."

Nukilik snorted her disappointment. "Let's go."

"Put this on." Wangari offered up a large headset that fit snug around Nukilik's face. It was painted white. "Now you'll never miss one of Murdock's knock-knock jokes."

"In that case, you can have it back," Nuk grumbled.

A moment later the polar bear was in the water,

following the pangolin through the South Pole and Hawaiian habitats and back into the maze of tunnels beneath the dome.

"HQ is located in a forgotten backup chamber," Wangari explained. "It has something to do with ventilation throughout the Ark. Humans never go there, so we have it all to ourselves. We call it the Big Top. It's a perfect location for us to train and plan missions."

A thick metal door blocked their path. Wangari knocked on it—twice. The narwhal answered via their headsets with a snicker and a cheeky, "Who's there?"

"Murdock, just because you don't have a neck doesn't mean I can't find a nerve to chop," Wangari warned.

The door buzzed and popped open. A fierce wind threw the hatch wide. Wangari jumped over the high threshold and Nukilik followed. She had to lean her full weight against the door to shove it closed behind her. The wind died out.

They descended a long ramp into the darkness and found themselves in the interior of a vast circular space with concrete walls and a high conical ceiling. The room's center was occupied by a large pool.

A tusk breached the water's surface, then Murdock's

beady eyes emerged along the sides of his bulging head. "Welcome to the Big Top!" the marine mammal declared cheerfully. "Center ring is home to the finest narwhal-infested swimming pool this side of the Amazon. We're working on the rat problem. But they dress like knights around here, so they're hard to vanquish." He winked playfully at Wangari.

"You call me a rat again," warned the pangolin, "and I'll cut off your tusk and carve it into toothbrushes."

"Sounds like something a rat would do," grumbled the narwhal.

"I'm impressed you can come and go between the aquarium and here," Nuk observed.

"I have ocean access too," Murdock boasted. "I'm just small enough to get through the transport tunnels to the bay. This saltwater pool has something to do with the Ark's cooling system. And the room itself is supposed to equalize pressure throughout the dome."

Wangari pointed to a wall of computer monitors. "Along with Murdock's interface in this pool and back in the Ark's aquarium, we can control all automated functions and watch anything that goes on inside the dome."

She hopped up on a desktop console and tapped a

series of keyboard inputs. A dozen giant high-definition flat-screens anchored to the curved wall flashed to brightness. "There's a lot we can do at once," the pangolin continued. "Surveillance, diagnostics, stay on top of newsworthy global events, stream nature documentaries—"

"Don't forget cat videos," Murdock interjected.

Wan pressed on. "We can access library books and scholarly journals, order supplies like 3D printing alloys, fuel for the jet, etcetera. We piggyback our orders onto scheduled deliveries using existing vendors already contracted with the Ark."

Nukilik removed the bone from her mouth, squinting into the dark along the far side of the pool. "Where's this aircraft?"

"Keep going," Wangari instructed. "You'll see."

Motion-activated lights flickered on as Nukilik walked past the pool. A large shape materialized out of the darkness, set out from the curvature of the wall. Nukilik walked a slow lap around the entire vehicle. The exterior was painted all black with some red trim, making it hard for the eye to follow. A massive *E* encircled with an arrow was painted on the hull beneath the wings.

"She's state of the art," Wan said proudly. "We call her *Red Tail* like a red tailed hawk."

Throughout her life, Nuk had occasionally seen airplanes and helicopters flying above the Great Realm but never up close. *Red Tail* looked like a combination of both.

Murdock confirmed her thinking. "Those propellers are extra large. The wings can rotate—to orient the props either forward, like on a typical airplane, or up, like helicopter blades."

"You stole this without anyone noticing?" Nukilik asked them.

"I'm sure the loss went noticed." Wangari chuckled. "But no one thought to blame a wallaby and an orangutan. Like I said, long story." She escorted Nuk back to the computer station.

"What's that?" Nukilik pointed at something that looked like a giant ball on the screens.

"Seriously?" asked Murdock. The narwhal tried to whistle, though it came out more like a failed trumpet blast. "You don't know what that is?"

"Don't embarrass her!" Wangari snapped at the narwhal. She turned to Nuk. "It's okay. It's called a globe.

Or a map. That's Earth. Our planet. Come here. Look. You can orient the image with this track pad. Center the globe however you like. This is the Arctic, where you'll focus your search to find home."

Nukilik gaped. "The world is on the surface of a giant ball?"

Wangari nodded proudly, as if she were responsible for making it. "As far as we know, it's the only corner of the universe that actually contains life, so we ought to take care of it, yeah?"

Nuk suddenly felt a stab of humiliation for how little she knew about life outside of the Great Realm.

She got the hang of navigating the virtual globe quickly. There were so many different land masses! Wan and Murdock spoke the names of the various continents as she slowly spun the image around. She studied the labels as the animals read them aloud, and she found herself seeing patterns in the symbols. She figured out what the next place was called before they said it: "Ja-pan?"

"You nailed it!" Murdock cheered. "You'll be reading in no time."

Far more fascinating to her, though, was the globe

itself. "The Arctic is only a small part of the entire world," she realized. "Where are we now? The Galápagos?"

Wangari showed her. "Here. Very close to the equator, off the coast of a country called . . . wait for it . . . Ecuador."

"Such a tiny dot!" Nukilik couldn't stop exploring the map. "You're from Africa. Here?" she asked the pangolin.

Wangari nodded. With her own track pad, she drew a circle around a large area within the continent. "This is my species' home range," she said. "All the places where we can naturally thrive in the wild. Our range is shrinking and becoming fragmented, thanks to habitat destruction. It's the same issue with the ferrets in North America, here, and also with Arief's kind."

"And where is he from?"

"Sumatra," said a familiar voice. Arief had crept into the Big Top and snuck up behind Nukilik while she was distracted. "Sorry I'm late. I've been waiting with Hobbs for Jill's return. They still haven't released her back into the grassland hab. But I wanted to stop by here to see what you think of the place."

The polar bear acknowledged him with a respectful

nod. "It's a nice hideout," she said.

"I'm pushing to call it a lair," said Murdock from the pool.

Arief joined Nuk at the track pad and centered the map on the chain of large islands between southeast Asia and Australia. "My home was here." He pointed to one of the land masses at the center of the zoomed-in map. Then he swiped the map quickly to the south and indicated the western coast of Australia. "And this is where Willie was from."

Nukilik considered the location thoughtfully and then zoomed the map back out and centered it on the Arctic Circle. She was amazed by how far away Australia could be from her Great Realm, which no longer seemed so great in her eyes, at least in terms of size.

"What are all these things everywhere?" Nukilik asked, squinting to read some of the hundreds of names she was seeing as she turned the virtual globe. "San Francisco? Bangkok? Mumbai?"

"They're cities," Murdock spouted enthusiastically.

"What are cities?" Nukilik asked.

"Um," the narwhal thought carefully. "Kind of like . . . giant nests? Or colonies! Where humans live closely together in structures they build, called buildings."

"He's not doing a very good job explaining," Wangari concluded.

"Have you ever seen an anthill?" asked Arief.

"No," the polar bear answered flatly.

She chewed on her bone while the others wrestled with the awkward silence that followed. "But I have seen seal colonies. And musk ox herds. And flocks of birds taking over rocky islands. And I've seen buildings now. I think I get it. Cities are where humans swarm."

She returned to gnawing on her bone while studying the globe. "Where are all the places you've visited as a team?"

Wangari took control of the map. "We've run a handful of missions so far. One in the Americas, one in Europe, here." She pointed to a place called the Black Sea. "And a quick one here in Madagascar."

"Hmm," Nukilik grunted to herself. She backed away from the computer bench to gather in all the monitors at once. "And you've made a difference for the animals in these places?"

"We are just starting out, but yes, I believe we are

making a positive difference," Arief insisted. "Definitely. There are plenty of problems to tackle, and the animals we help usually need assistance for different reasons."

"What do you mean?" asked Nukilik.

"Take my home, Sumatra, for example. In Indonesia. Our forests are all but gone, thanks to human-caused habitat destruction. They burn down our trees and plant giant farms of their own food instead. They also hunt my kind and steal us from our families, to sell us as pets. My guess is that your situation in the Arctic was totally different."

Nukilik pondered this for a moment. She had seen humans regularly but not frequently throughout her life, and when she saw them, they weren't busy destroying habitat or converting her territory into farms. Polar bears were having trouble because the weather wasn't working the way it always had, and her food sources were more and more difficult to find each year. "I haven't seen the humans actively destroying the Great Realm," she admitted to the group. "They don't hunt us or drive us out. But something is wrong where I live, all the same."

"Oh, it's the humans, all right," grumbled Murdock. "What we're experiencing in the Arctic are effects from something called climate change. The humans are altering the very atmosphere so that sunlight gets turned into too much heat energy. That's making global weather patterns change, and it's causing too much ice to melt at the poles, and that's why our whole natural food web is out of whack, Nuk."

"The humans are making the weather change?" Nukilik looked up at the big world depicted on the screens and felt her shoulders grow heavy. "If they can change climates all over this massive globe—how can you possibly stand up to them, about anything?"

"By trying," Arief said. He stared into Nukilik's eyes, his voice growing louder as he spoke. "By showing up. And never giving up. Everything starts off small. The key is to take the first step—and then keep going. When Willie and I were starting out, we realized that with our new abilities, we had the power to do more than just focus on ourselves. We couldn't turn our backs to that purpose."

"I didn't start off small," Murdock said. "When I was born, I weighed twice as much as you ever will."

No one laughed. "Shut your blowhole," scolded Wan.

“I still don’t see what good you’re doing,” Nukilik challenged.

The orangutan turned away, taking special care not to meet Nukilik’s eyes. “You have work to do, Nuk. I suggest you begin your search. I’m going back out to wait with Hobbs for Jill’s return.” He dragged his knuckles as he left.

Nuk stared after Arief as he walked away. She felt bad for putting him in a sour mood. She knew he was upset that she wasn’t joining the team. But she couldn’t let Arief’s ambitions distract her from what *she* needed to do. While Arief’s words had struck a chord, she had her own broken dreams to deal with. Saving the world one critter at a time was not her job.

Nukilik sat down on the bench seat at the computer terminal. With Wangari’s help, she devised a plan to scan the coasts everywhere polar bears lived. After a round of intense questions and answers, the pangolin narrowed their search to an area that also included the range of the Atlantic puffin bird and the routes of three different shipping lines that painted their vessels with colors Nuk described.

Still, the resulting map area was very large.

"You've got your work cut out for you!" Wangari noted. "I'm going back to the cube for some shut-eye. I'm nocturnal by nature, but you wore us out today, my new friend."

"Thank you for everything," said Nukilik.

"Be sure to get back to your hab before daybreak."

"Copy that."

Wangari snatched up her utility harness and strapped it on, adjusting the fit and making sure the tools tucked into it were snug.

Before leaving, she stopped. "You know," she said, choosing her words carefully, "you may think what we're doing doesn't make a difference. But we're helping you, aren't we? I wonder what difference that makes."

The pangolin let herself out without waiting for an answer.

Nukilik heaved a deep sigh but settled as comfortably as she could into her seat. The narwhal had also departed at some point, leaving her alone in the Big Top. Gnawing at her bone, she worked throughout the night, studying zoomed-in aerial views of coastlines from Canada to Greenland. She was confident she would eventually recognize an image of her home, and then the Endangereds would help her get there. If they wanted to act all smug and hoity-toity about it, fine: Nukilik could put up with it.

I'm on my way, Mamma.

That was all that mattered.

But her mind and her eyes sometimes wandered. She kept stealing glances at *Red Tail* across the way, and zooming her globe out to marvel at other parts of the Earth.

CHAPTER THIRTEEN

ARIEF

(Pongo abelii)

Arief woke from a restless sleep just as the sun's first rays were striking the top of the glass dome high above the cube; the effect was beautiful. Light reflected downward as if a massive crystal chandelier had been turned on. It lit up the dim jungle canopy, which scattered the light into a million hues of green and sent the colorful birds into fits of excitement. And then the moment passed. The sun rose enough to wash out the spotlight effect that had beamed into the cube. The birds calmed down a bit, as if they were disappointed.

The orangutan pursed his lips. It seemed that nothing beautiful could last forever.

"How can you possibly stand up to them, about anything?"

"I still don't see what good you're doing."

The polar bear's questions last night hadn't been mean-spirited or mocking. Nukilik was asking honest questions. And the truth was—Arief didn't have answers.

"What *are* we doing?" he asked the trees, stretching awake. *Running around the globe like bushy-tailed circus clowns, telling ourselves we're making a difference?*

"We're doing what we can," he answered aloud, pushing away his grim mood. "And that's more than Nukilik can say."

But that wasn't fair, and he knew it. Arief had hoped to convince the polar bear to join the Endangereds. But what more could he do? Nukilik had every right to tread her own path.

"Don't let the naysayers get you down," he cautioned himself.

But that wasn't all that was putting him in a rotten mood. Jill hadn't returned to her hab last night and not knowing her whereabouts was weighing on him and

Hobbs both. Arief had checked in with Hobbs briefly before heading to bed. The ferret was more nervous than he was letting on.

I'd better get over there to check on him, he decided.

"Your disposal is at my disposal," said an all-too-familiar voice approaching from a nook behind the waterfall.

"Go away, Poop-E," Arief grumbled.

"Why are you not making an offering?" the poo-bot asked. "Are you constipated?"

"No!" Arief cleared his throat. There was no point in yelling at the cube-shaped machine.

"Do you need more fiber in your dietary supplements?"

"I'm just not ready yet, Poop-E. Come back later."

Murdock had tried once to reprogram the pushy poo-bots at Arief's request. Big mistake. After a week of the bots being on the fritz, the entire Ark had acquired a horrible odor. The only thing Murdock had managed to accomplish was to sneak some new language routines into the code.

Poop-E rolled back into its nook, head hung low. "Like I want to put up with your crap, anyway."

Human footsteps approached along the cube's gravel path. Dr. Caitlyn Fellows came around the bend, alone, carrying her clipboard. It was routine for her to pass through the cube and the other habitats on occasional mornings she was here. Hopefully she had just dropped Jill off at the grassland. Arief would find out in a minute.

Meanwhile, he felt a flutter of affection when the vet came into view. He liked Dr. Fellows. Her concern for the animals, both here and out in the wild, was plain to see. Arief wondered, and not for the first time, if he should just reveal his hyperintelligence to her and trust that she would react in all the right ways.

But he had put trust in humans before and had come to learn that doing so was usually a mistake.

"Good morning, Pongo!" she called over, her face brightening as she spied him sitting cross-legged in one of his usual spots. She readjusted her glasses up onto her nose and draped some of her dangling curly hair behind her ear.

Arief put a hand on top of his head and stuck his tongue out. He wasn't in the mood for anything goofier, and Dr. Fellows generally wasn't as amused by his displays as were other visitors.

"Just waking up?" she asked. She stood opposite him, scanning him up and down, and wrote a few notes on her clipboard. "I'll let you get back to doing your thing. Mr. Gooding will be by with your breakfast in a bit. Say, you haven't seen Pinecone loose anywhere, have you?"

A jolt of alarm shot up Arief's spine. He nearly revealed his surprise with a jerk but managed to remain still. Pinecone was the name the humans had given to Wangari.

The pangolin was never late for morning rounds.

The vet chuckled at herself for bothering to ask the question. "I'm sure she's in there somewhere, burrowing, maybe. Never you mind about it. I'll miss you, Pongo! I'm headed off on another trip for a bit. But I'll see you when I get back, okay? Things are going to be quiet here for a few days with the construction crews off-island for the holiday, but you'll still get fed by the automatics. Bye!"

Arief knew the pangolin wasn't burrowed out of sight during the morning walk-through. If Dr. Fellows hadn't seen her, it meant she was out of her cage. The vet walked away and Arief immediately knuckled over to a nook in his enclosure's rock formation. He reached for his headset. "Wan, do you copy?"

He waited. No one answered.

"Hey, guys. Check in, please. Over?"

The silence stretched out just long enough for him to gather a sense of panic, and then a click came. It was Murdock, acting grouchy. "A bit early for roll call, isn't it?"

"Copy," said Arief. "Wan? Hobbs? Jill? Nukilik? Come in, please."

"Wan's not with you?" asked Murdock.

"I'll double-check," Arief said. "Meanwhile, can you visually confirm Nuk's in her hab?" He raced out of the back of his enclosure and circled around to the cube's neighboring pangolin exhibit. A gentle rain started just as he reached the spot along Wangari's fencing where they usually hung out together.

Wan wasn't there.

Arief could understand why Dr. Fellows was curious but unconcerned: there were plenty of places where the pangolin could be hiding, burrowed, or simply camouflaged. But Arief was convinced the enclosure was empty.

"Wan, where are you?" he pleaded, into both the cage and his headset. "Hobbs?"

"Nukilik's accounted for," Murdock confirmed

after another moment of worrisome silence. "She's dead asleep. Must've been doing her search all night long."

Well, that's good, at least, Arief thought. "Copy that."

"I'm checking the security feeds," Murdock reported. "Grassland looks empty of ferrets. The prairie dogs are lazing around, happy as house cats. I'd think they'd be more on guard if either of those bandit-faced mustelids was on patrol."

"I don't understand," Arief murmured. "How can all three of them be missing? They'd be on their radios if they were out and about."

"Not looking good," Murdock agreed. "Want me to check the Big Top?"

"Yes, if you can do it quickly, go for it." This was a bad time for any of them to be at large in the Ark, as morning feeding routines would start any minute, with bots and the vet assistant making the rounds everywhere at once.

The narwhal gurgled a series of goodbyes. "Copy, copy. Ten-four. Roger. Out. Over."

Arief waited. The silence was difficult to put up with. Every minute or so he tried the radio again, hoping for an answer. It was altogether possible that Wan, Hobbs, and Jill were somewhere safe—in the tunnels, maybe, where concrete was blocking their radio signals.

But he was losing hope.

The minutes seemed like hours. Murdock chimed in. "I'm at the Big Top. No sign of anyone. They're not here."

And then the minutes turned into real hours.

Arief was nearly mad with worry now, but there was little he could do. A maintenance crew had entered the cube to feed the birds and other rain forest critters and to troubleshoot the sprinkler system—which the Endangereds had caused to "malfunction" on purpose yesterday. The orangutan was stuck where he was, forced to interact with them every few minutes as they took turns trying to play with him through the wire netting of his enclosure.

Felix Gooding came with food, only visiting for a moment before moving on. Arief ate, but only as a matter of necessity. His stomach was not feeling good.

Poop-E returned, pestering him. "Where's the beef, *muchacho*? Time to ante up!"

Highly annoyed, Arief provided the bot with an offering to make it go away for the day.

He stole updates from Murdock as often as he could, though the narwhal was usually unavailable for comment, no doubt being plagued by humans himself.

"It's interesting," Murdock pointed out during one of their brief check-ins. "A crew has been through the grassland a couple of times. No one seems concerned that the ferrets are AWOL."

Arief thought about that, and he found it interesting too. *Wherever they are, the humans know about it.*

An image of his friend Willie came to mind. His small wallaby's body. His cute, furry face. Quokkas were famous for their humanlike smiles. You could almost mistake them for large rodents except for their natural charm. Willie had been whisked away from the Ark, without even a chance to say goodbye. And Arief had never seen him again.

Finally, the human activity throughout the habs died down, as it usually did around lunchtime. Arief made an executive decision. "Wake the polar bear," he radioed to Murdock. "I'm coming to you."

He ventured through the grassland on his way to the Arctic exhibits, pausing for a long moment to confirm that the ferrets were indeed missing. He called out for them to answer, but they never did. Only the prairie dogs replied, yipping in a wave of glee throughout the habitat.

"The villainous overlords are *gone*," one of the prairie dogs told the orangutan, its dark eyes smirking up at him. The creature looked nothing like a dog. Instead, it resembled a cross between a giant chipmunk and an earless rabbit. A drab tan in color, it sat tall on its haunches.

"Yip!" agreed another. "We've got the run of the place now! Ha-*ha*!"

Silly, nervous little things, Arief thought. *Perfectly harmless, though.* A vision of one of these rodents going hyper crossed his mind. He turned away, shuddering.

Ignoring the chanting colony, he entered the tunnels through a disguised stairway. Several minutes later, he huddled up with Nukilik in her hab. The narwhal was hanging out near the moat's gate.

"Did you locate your home?" Arief inquired.

"Not yet," Nukilik grumbled, struggling through a yawn. "I worked all night on it. There's still so much ground to cover."

"It's a daunting task," Arief conceded. "You'll have to

stay at it, I imagine. Meanwhile, we have a problem." He explained the situation.

"I'll go look for them," Nukilik immediately said. She even rose to jump in her pool.

Arief got in her way. "Wait. Let's think this through a little before we risk making the situation worse."

"Think it through?" growled Nukilik. "What's there to mull over? Our friends are missing. Let's go find them."

Arief noted how Nukilik had used the word "our." But he didn't linger reflecting on it. "We need a plan."

Nuk snorted. "That's what my mother always says."

"I checked the computers," said Murdock. "I can't find anything official in the logs about the three of them. We might have better luck if we go into the offices and snoop around."

This idea was met by a long silence. The obvious challenge was plain for all three of them to see.

"Wangari and the ferrets have always been our spies," Arief pointed out. "With so many humans on-site for construction, we're too big to slip into the Admin wing unnoticed."

"I'll do it," Murdock volunteered. "I'll slither in and then inchworm out, disguised as a mop handle."

Arief tried to picture that and rewarded the narwhal with a short laugh. "Noble as your offer is," he said, "I guess it'll have to be me. I'll find a jacket and a hat to put on. Murdock, you can be my eyes and ears over the feeds."

"I could create a diversion," Nukilik suggested. "Maybe eat a penguin? I've been wondering how they'd taste." She bit down on her bone and gave the orangutan a wink.

Arief couldn't tell if she was joking or not. "Please don't eat the residents," he warned. "But a distraction might be necessary to clear out the Admin hall."

"I'll think of something," Nukilik reassured them.

Arief nodded his approval. His heart rate quickened at the thought of the risk they were about to take. But a grin came to his face all the same. "Endangereds," he said, "time to gear up for action."

"Now, hold on just a minute," protested Nukilik. "I never said I was an—"

But Arief was already busy swinging up the cable toward the skywalk, off to the janitor's closet where he knew he'd find the perfect costume to wear.

CHAPTER FOURTEEN

MURDOCK

(Monodon monoceros)

Great Blue Abyss, *I'm not gonna get any sleep tonight.*

Murdock hovered with neutral buoyancy near the bottom of his aquarium, studying one of his command center displays. Up until a second ago, the black-and-white video feed recording the topside of his own habitat had looked down upon an empty exhibit. The water was relatively calm. The petting platform and staging deck were quiet, and the two visible hallways retreating into shadows were still. But just now, a humanlike form appeared, lurking at the edge of the darkness in the left hallway. Slowly and on all fours, it slunk forward toward the tank, hugging the wall.

To Murdock, it looked like the image of a man wearing an orange gorilla suit and a hooded yellow raincoat and galoshes, pretending to walk like a spider. He shuddered.

"Arief, please tell me that's you coming down corridor B," he pleaded, "and not a monster out of a Stephen King book."

"Who?" whispered the orangutan.

"An author. He writes about rabid dogs and cosmic turtles and shape-shifting clown spiders."

"I'm almost in position," said Arief, giving the camera a knowing tip of the latex raincoat hood.

"Are you sure this is a good idea?" Murdock had to ask. "That outfit doesn't conceal you very much. Just kind of makes you look like a hairy banana slug." *And that's being kind.*

"No. But we're short on time, and we're out of options. Every minute that goes by without answers reduces our chances of finding our friends."

"Okay, but . . ." Murdock fell silent. Arguing his point was of no use. His point being that Arief had made himself far more attention-grabbing and obvious—and terrifying—by trying to put on a costume. A sigh bubbled out of the narwhal's blowhole. The Endangereds were going to have to get better at the art of disguise. Especially if the polar bear came around on the subject of joining their posse. But that was a conversation for later. Right now, Murdock resigned himself to his job, which was to make absolutely certain that Arief had a one hundred percent clear shot of reaching the office computers without being seen, or even glimpsed, by anyone, ever.

Otherwise, a poor human that stumbled upon him might have a heart attack, and then things would get really complicated.

Murdock floated up to his command center's next level of touch screen displays and swiped his small fin at the glass several times, navigating the interface to bring up the video feeds of all the corridors and rooms in the Ark's Administrative wing.

The area was pretty empty at the moment. Everyone seemed to be gathering in the conference room, which had been recently decorated with streamers and ribbons and balloons. Cakes and beverages and assorted finger foods were arranged on tables. Murdock occasionally caught sight of a human cub darting here and there among the mingling adults. That was unusual, he noted, but not unheard of. A few of the *Homo sapiens* were moving their bodies around to the beat of something the humans called a song—which was ridiculous, because humans knew zilch about singing.

You want a real song? Ask a whale.

Anyway, some sort of human cultural festival was commencing, Murdock figured. This made sense, as one of the crew types whose job was to scrape barnacles off Murdock's back had mentioned in passing that the Ark was going to empty out for the next several days thanks to a holiday. Murdock hadn't cared enough to remember the details. He'd been in the throes of ecstasy as the guy scratched his back.

"I'm in position," the hairy fisherman from the orange lagoon reported. "It's really hard for me to walk only on my hind legs."

"It's okay," Murdock offered. "Go ahead and knuckle-walk. Be yourself. Your raincoat will hide your strides." *Not*, he thought.

"Copy that," Arief replied. He sounded ashamed.

"Always be yourself," Murdock continued. "Unless you can be a narwhal. Then always be a narwhal."

"Waiting for your signal," Arief said impatiently.

Hmmm, the narwhal thought. "Hold off a sec."

Murdock quickly scanned the other video feeds. He was thinking that Arief might actually have a good shot of reaching the computer room *right now*. The polar bear's planned distraction might have the opposite effect of what they were going for. "Hey, Nuk?" he gurgled.

"I'm ready," Nukilik said.

"Actually, I'm thinking maybe it's best if we—"

The polar bear started to howl.

Ouch! Startled by the volume and strength of the roar, Murdock involuntarily vented water out of the hole on the top of his head. The headphones shook loose from his tympanic membranes and drifted to the tank floor. He could still hear Nuk, though—through the water.

Murdock blubbered his frustration. *That antlerless moose needs to learn how to follow directions!*

The wail sustained itself in one long note. As Murdock listened, even down here, he caught a hint of sadness and desperation in Nukilik's tone. His frustration turned to something more like sympathy. *That gal's letting off some serious steam. Let her do her thing.*

A tinny, crackled "burp" rose from below to meet his senses. It was something he felt along his tusk as much as he heard it. He could tell: the vibration belonged to Arief's voice.

"Ah, beluga chum," Murdock cursed. His headset was resting ten meters down. He descended quickly to retrieve it. He'd gotten better at using his tusk to guide it back onto his head, but it still took time and effort. He knew he looked stupid—like a seal using a Hula-Hoop—but at least no one was watching.

Finally, the radio slipped into place.

"Is that my signal? Over? Should I move in?" Arief was asking repeatedly.

"Sorry. Dropped my unit when the howling started. Stay put," Murdock instructed, competing to be heard over the radioed yowling. "You've got a gaggle of *sapiens* approaching quickly." The whale vented again. "It would have been better if you sprang to action *before* Nuk started playing the bagpipes. I was trying to tell her to stay quiet."

"I hear them coming," Arief confirmed. "Now what?"

"Wait it out, I guess?" Murdock suggested. "They'll get back to their party if Nuk lays off. Nuk? Do you read?"

The polar bear didn't seem to be listening. He zoomed in on her camera image. Yup. She'd removed her headset, knowing the humans would come to investigate as soon as she began making noise. This was actually the right move on her part, but . . . how was he supposed to feed her instructions now?

We should have thought this through a little more.

He could surface and yell at her directly, but a few of the humans were already at her enclosure, consulting each other. Probably safest to wait it out.

Murdock waited. And waited. Nukilik wasn't letting up. Murdock was almost impressed with her lung capacity, until he remembered how awesome his own breather bags were. He shrugged and passed the time by clearing items off the touch screens—they had become a jumble of windows. He closed out his level-twenty Minesweeper game, the Dostoyevsky novel he was reading, the *How to Hack Satellites for Dummies* instruction manual he'd illegally downloaded, and the cat video he'd bookmarked.

More people were leaving the conference room party and trickling into the Ark. *Maybe this will work, after all,* he thought. "Be ready, Arief. You may have a window here in a sec. Over."

The last stragglers filed over to Nuk's habitat, leaving only three humans in the Admin wing. They seemed pretty occupied with their slices of cake. Murdock made an executive decision. "Go, go, go!"

On-screen, an upright orange carpet wrapped in yellow latex loped across the deck toward the Admin entrance hall. Murdock's eyes snagged on additional movement in the shadows. He quickly flipped to a new camera and made sense of what he was seeing: the little human cub was wandering alone up the corridor.

"No! Wait, wait, wait!" Murdock abruptly spouted at the ape.

No use. Arief was carried by momentum into the hallway before he saw the child for himself. By the time he skidded to a halt on his knuckles, he and the cub were face-to-face.

The great ape and the tiny toddler squared off, gawking at each other.

Oh, this'll go well.

The boy's face turned as pale white as a beluga's bum. His mouth opened. His lips trembled.

"Shh. You're going to be good," Arief told him. "I—"

Bad call. The boy responded to the orangutan's assurances by screaming at the top of his lungs.

Now there's *a pair of breather bags!* thought Murdock.

On the other video monitor, where a crowd had gathered to investigate the howling polar bear, heads suddenly turned back toward the offices. Nukilik abruptly fell silent, aware that something was off. The boy's cry of terror was now totally unmistakable, echoing far and wide, audible even through the water.

On yet another screen, the remaining cake-eating humans dropped their food and rushed toward the conference room door, which opened onto the hallway.

Several snafus were now in mid snaf. "Get out of there!" Murdock spurted.

The frozen ape found his arms and legs and bolted back toward the aquarium. He was a yellow flash on the open deck, disappearing down the next dark hallway just as the crowd stampeded into view.

"How'd I do?" Nukilik asked over the radio. Murdock saw from his monitor that she was crouched, speaking into the headset while it was hidden among some rocks. A few of the humans lingered near her habitat, discussing something—probably wondering if it was safe to leave her alone. It was only now that Murdock realized Dr. Fellows was nowhere among the agitated *sapiens*. That wasn't particularly significant, but he did briefly wonder where she was before his mind refocused on the task at fin.

Arief growled from somewhere hidden, "How are we supposed to do this? Turns out we're helpless without our smaller team members."

"We botched it," Murdock agreed.

"The kid was so young. I thought it'd be okay to speak to him. I was just as surprised as he was. I wasn't thinking straight."

"Nope. But don't beat yourself up," Murdock said. He needed a breath of air and rose quickly to grab one.

"Wait, what?" Nukilik growled hoarsely. "All that was for nothing?"

"Well," Murdock started, his emotions getting the better of him as he ascended toward the surface, "you need to be a better listener. I was trying to tell you to abort. There's no I in team, you know."

"Cut the chatter, you guys," Arief insisted. "Let's keep the line open in case we get another shot at going in."

Murdock lifted his head above the water, stealing a peek at the humans down the long hallway, gathered around a trembling boy. The human cub was trying to tell everyone what he'd seen.

"It w-was Curious George, Mom! B-bu-but he was gigantic. He tried to eat me. H-h-he told me I was g-going to—going to taste good." He started crying as he remembered his nightmare encounter.

"Um, I don't think we're going to get another shot at this," Murdock said.

"Well, I give up," snapped Nukilik. "I tried to help. But you're right: this type of work is for the critters."

"Come in? Anyone? Over."

"I said, 'Cut the chatter'!" Arief barked in frustration.

"Arief! It's me. Wan."

A stunned silence fell over the comm for several seconds. Finally, Arief ventured a bewildered reply. "Wan? Wait. Is that really you? Where are you?"

The response was unintelligible and fizzled out.

Murdock abandoned the surface and dove fast. "Sounds like a weak signal," he explained. "I can boost it." He swam down to his command center and used his touch screens to tweak a series of broadcast settings.

The connection improved. Wan's voice rematerialized. "Can you hear me? Over?"

"Copy. We've got you back!" said Murdock. "Go on."

"Thank the ancestors, we're finally getting through. I've been trying to explain. I'm with Hobbs and Jill. We're in a place called . . . Hold on, let me look it up again. I keep forgetting the name." The pangolin could be heard asking a question and getting a muffled response from one of the ferrets. During the pause, Murdock kept fidgeting with various virtual dials on the display. The signal continued to strengthen, which was good, because Murdock wouldn't have believed he was hearing the pangolin correctly, otherwise.

"I've got it straight, now," she said. "We're in a land called Colorado. In the southwestern United States. The folks around here call this place the Four Corners."

A long silence followed.

"Do you read, over?" Wangari asked.

Murdock was the first to formulate a reply. "Whaaaat?"

"We're going to need your help," Wangari told them.

Murdock was already executing a search on the map he'd opened. United States. Colorado. Four Corners. There it was: a place where four states met at the corners. Utah, Colorado, Arizona, and New Mexico. More than three thousand miles away from the Galápagos. "Wan, what are you even doing there? How'd you get there so fast?"

Wangari could be heard taking a deep breath. "I'll try to explain," she began. "You see, a funny thing happened on my way to bed last night. . . ."

CHAPTER FIFTEEN

WANGARI

(Phataginus tetradactyla)

"You know," Wangari told Nukilik, "you may think what we're doing doesn't make a difference. But we're helping you, aren't we? I wonder what difference that makes."

The polar bear offered no response.

Wan left headquarters and closed the hatch with a shove, pushing hard. Her long, armored tail dragged behind her as she ascended the darkened tunnel toward the Ark surface. She had done her best to bottle up her bad mood while helping Nukilik start her search on the computers, but the polar bear's attitude had finally gotten under her very thick skin.

She accepts our help and in the same breath criticizes what we're doing.

Wan tried to shrug it off. Some animals were just difficult by nature. Especially top predators. But she couldn't quite shake her gloom.

In addition, her utility harness was rubbing her the wrong way. She lifted it and made a few adjustments as she walked, switching her suction cup launcher from one hip to the other. *Can't wait to get this thing off and grab a few z's.*

She reached the stairway leading to the grassland exhibit and mounted the steps slowly. She came out into the open just in time to glimpse Arief waving goodbye to Hobbs.

The orangutan turned to enter the cube, no doubt heading off to bed for the night.

Far above, the ceiling panels of the dome let in starlight and the faint glow of a half moon. Crickets fiddled in the tall grasses. The ferret stood on his back legs near a prairie dog mound and scanned his habitat with a forlorn expression. Ferrets didn't dig burrows of their own—they moved into a prairie dog's home after, um, eating them. They *literally* ate their prey out of house and home. It seemed to Wan to be a bit of a harsh practice, but when it came to the great animal kingdom, she knew, each species had their own ancient way, and she wasn't one to judge. From an ant's point of view, a pangolin was Godzilla, after all.

Wan crept forward and stood in the middle of the gravel path, watching Hobbs stare off into the distance.

It was clear to the pangolin that Hobbs was alone—and out of sorts. The humans hadn't returned Jill to the habitat yet. *That's not good*, thought Wan. She debated whether or not to approach Hobbs and ask him for an update. He might appreciate the distraction. On the other paw, it might be best to leave him alone so he could get a good night's sleep.

The pangolin's hearing wasn't her sharpest asset, so when she suddenly heard the approach of footsteps, it was almost too late. She rolled off the path into the tall prairie grasses and froze there, wrapped into a ball. Her headset had come off, but it rested too far away for her to reach after it. Once the footsteps went by, she uncurled herself, readjusted her crimped harness, and stole a peek above the grass stems.

The footsteps belonged to Dr. Fellows, and she was holding a pet carrier. A wave of relief washed over the pangolin. Finally, Jill was back!

But her relief quickly transformed into a stab of dread. Dr. Fellows entered the fenced-off exhibit and crouched near Hobbs, who looked on expectantly. When she rose, she was holding a long pole with a net at the end. Caught off-guard, Hobbs never had a chance. The vet nabbed him with one swoop and dropped him into the carrier, quickly slamming it shut.

The vet wasn't here to release Jill. She was here to capture Hobbs!

"Sorry for being rough, buddy," Dr. Fellows told her new prisoner. "I didn't want to tranq you unless I had to, but I know how quick you can be."

The vet exited the enclosure and set off down the path. Wangari ducked to avoid detection, but kept her eyes locked on the carrier as they passed. Hobbs made a chirp of protest but didn't offer any struggle. Maybe he was expecting that he would be brought to Jill.

Wan wasn't going to take that theory for granted. *I'm going to keep an eye on you*, she mentally promised her friend. She stayed in the grasses but wove quickly through them in a low crouch as she tracked the pair.

Dr. Fellows followed the meandering path out of the grassland and into the forest mountain pass habitat. She walked at a clip, and Wan had to hustle to keep up. She followed the vet out of the empty mountain exhibits, through the Hawaiian Island and polar regions, past Murdock's tank, and into the hallway leading to Dr. Fellows's lab. Wangari kept to the shadows wherever possible, hopping from one fake rock to another, running along narrow handrails, and occasionally dive-rolling to the ground. She risked staying in the open a few times to let Hobbs know she had his back, on the off chance he was watching through the tiny breathing holes in his carrier.

Wangari was surprised when Dr. Fellows marched past the door to her lab and kept going.

Well, this is odd. More than odd, maybe. Mental alarm bells sounded in her head.

Wan reached up to her ear, ready to put a call out to Arief. But she hadn't retrieved her headset from the grasses. *Termites!* she cursed. She considered going back to get it, but dismissed the idea. It was far more important right now to keep tabs on Hobbs.

When the vet exited the Ark and started approaching a whirring plane waiting at the end of the island's short runway, Wangari finally understood what was happening.

Oh, no. They're sending him away!

Wan darted through the closing door and bolted out into the dark open. The night air was damp and breezy. She watched the vet and Hobbs stride farther away toward the plane and felt panic rising. There was no cover between the building's edge and the plane, except for a luggage truck that sat on the tarmac beside the aircraft.

At least it's dark, Wan told herself. Still, that much open space was terrifying to a pangolin. She flexed her armored plates and rallied herself. "You can't lose him now. Just get this over with."

She fished a pair of brass-framed goggles out of her harness and wrapped them around her eyes. Then she galloped for the luggage truck, imagining flocks of owls and prides of bush cats running her down. She knew her fears were ridiculous, but she was glad that, even after all this time as a hyper, much of her natural instinct remained intact.

Wangari reached the luggage truck and dove through the curtain. She rested on a tipped-over suitcase and caught her breath.

"Are you on this flight?" she heard a man ask Dr. Fellows. They shouted back and forth to each other over the loud whine of the spinning propeller blades.

"No. I'm not even packed yet. I'll leave in the morning after I wrap a few things up."

Wan peeked through the curtain on the far side of the luggage truck and watched as Dr. Fellows handed the carrier holding Hobbs to the pilot.

"Make sure he stays comfortable. And *warm*," Dr. Fellows instructed. "Put him next to the other one. They're mates. It'll help keep them calm for the trip."

"Got it," replied the man, hopping into the plane and moving out of sight toward the cargo space at the back with Hobbs's carrier gripped in his hand.

Jill's there too! Where are they going?

The cargo door at the back of the plane closed automatically. The plane's motors began to speed up, pulling the aircraft forward. Dr. Fellows was already half the distance back to the Ark, waving. She turned her back and headed for the door.

There was no time to think. Wan unholstered her suction cup device, clipped the end of it onto her harness, pointed, and pulled the trigger.

The sucker cup struck the hull of the plane and held fast. Wangari was yanked violently forward. She grunted and curled up as tightly as she could, bounce-dragging along the pavement as the airplane gathered speed.

And I was worried about an owl a minute ago?

Suddenly she was airborne, dangling from the cable extending out of the cup launcher. She uncurled herself, adjusted her goggles, and activated the cable pull, slowly drawing closer to the ascending plane.

Once she was within tongue's reach of the hull, she stopped. She located the nearest cargo bay panel and zapped her tongue at it. Then she pulled herself closer to the plane by coiling her tongue muscle. Easy as eating ants at a picnic.

The panel flapped open when she clawed at it. She hooked one of her powerful claws inside the craft and pulled herself aboard.

"Wan!" both ferrets shouted at once.

"I saw you following me," Hobbs said. "But I figured you went back! What are you doing?"

She stabilized herself and shut the hatch, then turned to greet Hobbs and Jill, lifting her goggles above her brow. The ferrets were on a low shelf against the wall, their individual carriers strapped into place. The rest of the shelves were mostly empty. This charter flight was just for them, it appeared. "I'm here to . . ." She drifted off, not really sure what she was doing here. "Rescue you?"

"I'm so glad to see you," Jill said. It was hard to tell the two ferrets apart aside from their voices—and the slight bulge along Jill's tummy. "I've been missing everyone a lot. I really wish we'd had a chance to say goodbye. But a rescue isn't necessary, Wan."

"What?" asked both Wangari and Hobbs together.

"I'm pregnant," Jill explained. "Litter of five, I heard them say."

"Well, we know that," Hobbs answered. "I shared the news with the others when they first carted you off."

"Hobbs, we have a lot to discuss," said Jill, holding paws with her mate as they reached through their carrier slats. "Their plan is to reintroduce us into the wild. And I want to make it work."

"Really?" asked Hobbs. "Are you sure?"

Whoa. Hold on. "Gang," Wan piped in, "I'm sorry, but remember what happened to Willie?"

"This is different, Wan. Willie was dropped off in a strange environment far away from home. I've overheard a ton of conversations between Dr. Fellows and the ranger who works at our reintroduction site. We're being reintroduced in our natural historic range. It's where we belong. We have a real shot at being wild again."

Wan nodded her understanding but remained silent. She had to think about this before getting into a fight with her friends over it. And she needed to speak with the rest of the Endangereds, as soon as possible.

The problem was, she had no radio. And it would be who knew how long until she had access to one. Until the flight landed, at the very least.

Wan squeezed the cage-door latches, letting the ferrets out of their carriers. She smiled, watching them reunite. Hobbs and Jill zigged and zagged throughout the cargo hold. They nuzzled noses and brushed against each other often. The ferrets seemed to relish their abilities to slither and leap, their spry bodies too full of natural energy and excitement to scamper anywhere directly.

Over time, everyone settled in, keeping the conversation light. Wan found a spot a respectful distance away. She drifted off to sleep listening to the ferrets discuss their situation with each other.

It wasn't until they landed in a town called Cortez, Colorado, that Wan finally had an opportunity to sneak into the empty cockpit of the plane and calibrate the radio to communicate with the satellite repeater Murdock had hacked into during a previous mission, giving them global communication capacity. She worked at the onboard dash frantically for several minutes, knowing that the pilot or someone else would return before long.

Everything was properly programmed now. She turned the dial one notch at a time, hearing nothing but static, until finally she snagged on the voice of the narwhal. ". . . don't think we're going to get another shot at this."

Yes! That's them! Wangari seized the moment, leaning forward to talk into the mic. "Big Top, this is Wangari. Anyone copy? Murdock? Arief? Hello?" She waited a moment and tried again. Still no answer. But the third time it worked.

"Come in? Anyone? Over."

"I said, 'Cut the chatter'!"

That was definitely Arief. Her chest relaxed. "Arief! It's me. Wan."

The comm went quiet for a moment, but Arief finally answered. "Wan? Wait. Is that really you? Where are you?"

"We just landed at an airport in the United States," Wan explained in a rush. "We've been flying all night. They're planning to reintroduce Hobbs and Jill into the wild in the next few days."

She waited, but no one responded. This struck her as odd. Maybe they hadn't heard. "Can you hear me? Over?"

The silence stretched on, but finally, an answer came.

"Copy. We've got you back!" said Murdock. "Go on."

"Thank the ancestors, we're finally getting through. I've been trying to explain. I'm with Hobbs and Jill. We're in a place called . . . Hold on, let me look it up again. I keep forgetting the name."

The pangolin called over to the ferrets who were back in their carriers. "What's this place called again?"

The ferrets shouted up answers.

She turned back to the mic. "I've got it straight, now. We're in a land called Colorado. In the southwestern United States. The folks around here call this place the Four Corners."

A long silence followed. "Do you read, over?" Wangari asked.

Murdock answered. "Whaaaat?"

"We're going to need your help," Wangari told them.

Murdock sounded genuinely overwhelmed and not just fake overwhelmed like he often pretended to be. "Wan, what are you even doing there? How'd you get there so fast?"

Wangari took a deep breath then spent the next several minutes updating everyone back at the Ark about all that had happened since last night.

She kept her eyes focused outside the windows as she talked, absently soaking in the strange environment surrounding the airport: a rural cityscape surrounded by low-lying hills peppered with strange, round trees and orange and red rocks. But really she was scanning for the return of the pilot. Just as she was starting to explain that the ferrets were interested in *staying* in Colorado, the pilot reappeared and approached the plane. Knowing it would spark an argument, she decided there wasn't enough time to reveal the ferrets' thinking just yet.

"Okay, gang, I'm going to have to go. They're coming. I'll check back in when I have new info. Meanwhile, I'll follow the ferrets wherever they're headed and make sure they're safe."

"Copy," said Arief. "We'll get there as quickly as we can. Endangereds, let's make tracks!"

CHAPTER SIXTEEN

NUKILIK

(Ursus maritimus)

It was late evening. Nuk was in search of her home on the computers in the Big Top, using the large wall displays to scan coastlines. Arief and the narwhal arrived to give the tilt-rotor aircraft a tune-up. Murdock checked satellite signals from his pool console, preparing for a radio conversation with the traveling animals. Wangari had radioed late in the afternoon and suggested they all check in after dark.

Nukilik was trying—and failing—to ignore the others as she continued her hunt.

She scrolled across coastline after coastline, straining to stay alert.

Her heart rate quickened.

That one mountain . . . it looked so familiar! It conjured up a memory from when she was very young: a place where she and her mother had eaten a musk ox while shooing away arctic foxes trying to steal nibbles.

I think I know this place.

She focused her search on the coastlines to either side of the recognizable mountain peak.

Don't rush. Scan the beaches slowly or you might miss something important.

She had to repeat it to herself over and over.

"Connection seems good," Murdock announced from the surface of the pool at the Big Top's center. "Do you copy, Wan?"

"I'm here with the ferrets." Wangari's voice echoed everywhere, coming out of speakers around the chamber's circular wall. Nukilik couldn't tune it out. She chomped on her bone in frustration. "Dr. Fellows just arrived here this evening. She's overseeing the reintroduction herself. We're at a ranger station in the hills. Everyone's gone for the night. Jill, Hobbs, and I have the place to ourselves now."

"Wan had to cling to the back of a jeep on bumpy roads for an hour this afternoon!" Jill proudly informed everyone. "She's been keeping good track of us."

"I took video of my stuntwork with the head cam I keep in my utility harness," Wan said. "Digital bread crumbs so I know how to get back to the airport. I'll send the footage over later, if you want to check it out."

"Ooh, yes, please!" exclaimed Murdock. "More uploads for my secret social media hashtag: 'pangolin-parkour'!"

"That better be a joke," warned Arief, pulling his head out from under one of *Red Tail*'s engine access panels.

"I'm converting the headset to a two-way radio as we speak," said Wan. "Then I can pump you a live feed of what I'm seeing."

Arief knuckled over to be within earshot of the workstation microphone. Nukilik was feeling downright crowded now. She clamped down harder on the bone as if it could get her some quiet.

"We'll be ready to fly shortly," the orangutan explained. "We have enough gas. We're gathering supplies and running the 3D printer on overdrive. I've done the calculations. It's going to take us a while to get to you. I'm wondering if you guys should hightail it now, hole up somewhere safe until we arrive. Meanwhile, Murdock will hold down the fort and run point during the extraction."

"You keep saying 'us' and 'we,'" Nukilik observed, not looking away from the monitors. "I'm not going anywhere, not unless you want to continue up to the Arctic."

"We don't have the gas for that yet," Arief stated flatly.

"I'm not staying behind," complained Murdock. "I'm going on the mission."

The orangutan scoffed. "It's a land job, Murdock. There isn't an ocean within five hundred miles. Get real."

"Arief?" asked Wan.

Murdock humphed. "We're a team. I go on missions. End of story."

Nukilik turned, chomped on her bone, and offered the narwhal a sly grin. "There's no I in team, remember?"

The narwhal spluttered. "Fair enough. But if you look a little harder, add an extra E, you can find an 'eat me' in there somewhere."

Nuk rubbed her tummy. "Is that a challenge? Don't think I couldn't. I've had your kind before, you know."

"Oh, yeah? Did my poor auntie taste any good?"

"Not at all. It was the most disgusting meal I can remember."

"Worse than a beluga, even?"

"Oh, yes. Definitely."

Murdock seemed crushed by this fact.

"Arief?" asked Wan again.

Arief got between the squabbling Arctic mammals, his expression all business. "You're staying behind, Murdock, and you're making sure the skeleton crew that's here over the holiday doesn't figure out the rest of us are AWOL."

"There's that word again: us," grumbled Nuk. "I'm not a part of this."

Murdock grew louder. "Come on, Arief! I'm not staying here to fling poo at the fussy bots again. You know what? Maybe I can print up some kind of exo-suit, so I can run around the Four Corners with you.

Or some kind of giant saltwater hamster ball. I bet I can download engineering schematics!"

"You work on that," Arief told him. "If it's fully functional an hour from now, you can 'beach ball' your way through Arizona, and Nukilik will hang back and run point instead. Agreed?"

"Arief?" Wan asked a third time, her voice growing impatient.

"Just because I'm staying doesn't mean I'm covering for the rest of you," Nukilik insisted, summoning up a new set of images for the computer displays. "I've got enough to do."

"ARIEF!" Wan yelled. Her voice crackled throughout the Big Top.

"What is it?"

"Our friends don't want to be extracted. They're not looking for a rescue. They want to stay in the Four Corners."

Nukilik's ears perked up. She locked eyes with Arief, who suddenly looked confused. "Repeat that, over. I don't think I heard it right," he finally said.

Jill's voice came over the speakers. "Being a part of the Endangereds has meant so much to us. But we're starting a family, Arief. We've got a shot at raising our kits in the wild. We need to seize this chance."

A long silence followed the announcement.

Nukilik swiveled on her stool and studied the narwhal and the ape. Murdock sank in the water to his eyes, as if to hide. Arief noticeably stiffened.

"What's wrong?" Hobbs challenged everyone. "You're acting like this is bad news. We're excited!"

"But, guys," said Murdock, rising in the water so he could speak clearly, "won't your family be safer here?"

Nukilik was thinking hard. She could see why Arief and Murdock were hesitant. But she understood exactly why the ferrets were enthusiastic. A chance to leave this place behind: it was all she wanted.

"I get it," offered Arief. "I see what you're after." He went up to the mic at the computer station and shifted his weight from one set of knuckles to the other. "But you've never been in the wild."

"You're right. We've been in captivity our whole lives," Hobbs admitted. "But we've got what it takes to succeed, especially as hypers, and—"

"I'm not questioning your ability to figure out your natural environment," Arief said. He rubbed his free hand through his hair. "I'm worried about the humans. Black-footed ferrets almost went extinct, you know."

"Yes, but our populations are on the rise now," argued Jill. "Black-footed ferret reintroductions are a scientific success story. It's an example of wildlife management that's working!"

Arief grunted and thumped his chest. Nukilik had never seen him this worked up. "The earliest ferret reintroductions were disastrous!" he argued. "The released ferrets died left and right because they were all bred from the same parents—they had no genetic diversity to fight off sicknesses or diseases. And ranchers and farmers purposefully killed off prairie dogs, your only food source, because their burrows destroyed crops and injured cattle. How are you going to feed your family if the locals keep getting rid of your menu?"

Hobbs answered, his voice patient but firm. "It's all true. But our human allies have come a long way since those early days. And Dr. Fellows wouldn't sign off on this if it were too risky. We heard the rangers say that the community around the Four Corners is excited we're moving in."

"I have a long history with humans," warned Arief.

"I know what happens. I'm glad Dr. Fellows is there, but she'll eventually leave. And humans don't change their ways easily, certainly not because scientists ask them to! This is riskier than you want to admit."

Wangari shared a low growl. "He may have a point," she said. "There's a local here, a guy named Murray Sheridan. He lives near the reintro site. They were going to do a big public ceremony with Hobbs and Jill but decided against it because they didn't want to tip this guy off that it was happening."

"Exactly," said Arief, pressing his knuckles into the ground and puffing his chest. "See? I'm not surprised."

"Okay," admitted Jill, "but . . . so . . . that's going to stop us from living out the rest of our lives where we belong?"

"If this Sheridan person finds out about you, he could take you out," Arief speculated.

Nukilik had heard enough. She squared shoulders with the ape. "What are you saying? Are you telling them they shouldn't go back to their home? Are you keeping them imprisoned here, the way you want to keep me?"

Arief looked at his hairy feet. He heaved a big sigh. Everyone waited. After a moment, he gave the polar bear a hard look. "These are my friends, Nukilik. Scientists measure their success in numbers. Perhaps there are thousands of black-footed ferrets across their natural range again. That's wonderful news. But how many died along the way? A *lot*. To me, Hobbs and Jill and their kits are not just numbers. They're my responsibility." He turned his gaze from Nuk to the nearest microphone. "I've lost one friend already. It scares me to think you and your kits might not survive this journey."

"It's not about you, Arief," Nukilik pressed him. "This is for them to decide."

"I know that," Arief said reluctantly.

"We want this," Jill repeated to everyone. "We know the risks. And we will miss all of you. But Nukilik is right."

Arief sat down hard on the ground beside the computer console. He rubbed at his chin. After a long while, he slowly nodded. When he finally rose to speak, he watched Nukilik closely. "It breaks my heart, Hobbs and Jill, to say farewell to more family. We *are* family, you know. But if you're ready to return to the wild, I won't stand in your way."

"Thank you, Arief. I know that wasn't easy for you

to say," said Jill. "It's not so easy for us either. We love the Endangereds. But this is our time."

The orangutan's expression remained stern. "Either way, I want to monitor this situation. Wan, I want you to watch the reintroduction closely, then sneak a ride back here with Dr. Fellows once we're sure everything is safe."

"That works," Wangari said over the airwaves. "The release will happen tomorrow. I'll have this headset cam operational by then, and I'll live stream what I see to you. We can all monitor together how it goes."

"I think this is the right move," offered Murdock. "I'm excited for our little friends. We'll need to maximize the satellite bandwidth for a high-def broadcast, but I'm on it."

The great ape gave Nukilik a searching look.

"This must be hard for you," Nuk said. She wasn't really feeling the urge to give him more credit than that.

Arief shook his head. "I only want what's best for all of us, Nukilik. But it's more difficult than you think—in most cases—to know exactly what that is."

CHAPTER SEVENTEEN

WANGARI

(Phataginus tetradactyla)

"Come in, Big Top," Wangari said. She used a claw to adjust her headset. "I'm in position. How's the feed look?"

"Vid's coming through nice and crisp," Murdock responded.

The pangolin grinned. After she'd found the radio at the wildlife management station and stripped it for parts last night, she'd gotten the circuitry to work on her head cam without much difficulty.

Her growing knowledge of how to create small

electronics filled her mind with possibilities. Insect drones, tracker beacons, digital picklocks, LCD filters and enhancements for her brass goggles, and so much more . . . her utility belt would be bursting at the seams before the next mission. Combined with Murdock's natural talents for coding and programming—and developing smartphone apps that could be paired with Wan's inventions—there was no limit to the spy tools they could create as time went on.

"I routed the feed onto the Big Top displays," said Murdock. "Looks gorgeous out there today, over."

"All quiet on the southwestern front," Wan told them. She was crouched on a low juniper branch on the hillside overlooking a meadow of sagebrush, bunch grasses, and other junipers. Her tail was wrapped around the alligator bark of the branch for added support. "Perfect Gunnison's prairie dog territory," she commented, turning her head in a wide arc to show those in the Galápagos the full landscape. "Which means—"

"Ideal ferret habitat," answered Arief in her ear. He still sounded skeptical, but maybe the orange guru's concern for their friends was softening.

Using binoculars she'd also swiped from the wildlife

management office, Wangari scanned a cage resting on a low wooden table, spying the silhouettes of Hobbs and Jill behind the steel bars. She had shared an emotional farewell with them early this morning, knowing it was possible they'd never be together again. Wan would miss the ferrets. But she was happy and excited for them too.

Personally, she couldn't imagine leaving the Endangereds behind. But she understood why Jill and Hobbs were choosing to move on and start their family here.

Wangari panned over and focused on the lone human, a wildlife management ranger with a name badge reading, "Officer J. Nez." Nez looked relaxed, fiddling with a camera and a tripod.

Wan glanced up at the sun, shielding her eyes. High noon would arrive anytime now.

"Reminds me of a gallows," Murdock intoned. "Where prisoners used to hang, back in the Old West."

Wan made small adjustments to the head cam's fit on her head, remembering that she was serving as the remote eyes and ears for the team back in the Galápagos. "Shush, now. That's not a good omen," she warned.

A jeep came over the nearby hill and parked next to the wildlife management truck. Both vehicles were positioned between Wan and the ferrets, which wasn't a bad thing: the pangolin now had a bit of cover if she needed to approach.

Dr. Fellows hopped out of the jeep, partially blocked from view, and strode toward the wildlife ranger. She shook Nez's hand. They huddled around the camera, making final arrangements.

Little did they know, the Endangereds had made arrangements of their own.

If something went wrong, Wan was ready to spring into action with her sucker cup launcher, a smoke canister, a micro-Taser with a single charge, and of course her substantial tongue-to-tail combat training.

A prairie dog off to the side of the parked vehicles poked its head out of its burrow and gave a call of alarm. Answering calls of alarm came chirping back from various locations.

"Yip!"

"Yip!"

Wangari had done her research: it was typical for prairie dogs to sound off from the entrances to their burrows. They were a social species, and their natural system of defense was to warn each other of approaching predators. Wan guessed the warning call was in response to a hawk hovering overhead.

She searched the cloudless sky and was a little surprised to find nothing of the sort up there.

That's weird, she thought. *What are they so nervous about?*

She shrugged, supposing it was possible they sensed a pair of natural predators—aka ferrets—in their midst.

"Wan, can you tilt your head back down so we can see the stage?"

"Sorry." The pangolin settled her focus again on the reintroduction activity.

Over by the ferrets, Officer Nez was pointing the camera at Dr. Fellows. He gave her a signal, and she spoke in an educational tone. The breeze carried the vet's voice up the hill, and the Endangereds listened in.

"Disease and habitat destruction brought the black-footed feet, which once numbered in the tens of thousands from Canada to Mexico, to the brink of extinction. In 1986, there were only *eighteen* black-footed ferrets left on the planet, none of them in the wild. Scientists have been breeding them in captivity since then and have attempted many reintroductions along the way.

Some of the early efforts ended with unfortunate setbacks. But today we're proud to announce that ferret populations across their historic range are stabilizing. Here, in the Four Corners region, our efforts to reestablish large prairie dog colonies as a food source for ferrets and other predator species are working. Each ferret will eat around one hundred prairie dogs a year. That's a lot of prairie dogs for a family of seven ferrets, which is what will be established here. But that's no problem! The Gunnison's prairie dog population around here is near maximum capacity, and local ranchers and farmers and residents throughout the area support the effort to balance the ecosystem through a natural approach."

Does she not know about this Sheridan guy? Wangari wondered, thinking back to all the materials she had seen in the wildlife office. Sheridan had been arrested recently for disorderly conduct. He'd been harassing local law enforcement, including wildlife rangers—even the local dogcatchers—for not doing their jobs. It was clear from what Wangari had read that Sheridan had problems. He'd told the police in one report: *"I hear them laughing at me. I know what they're saying. But I'll have the last laugh. You wait and see. With or without your help."*

A mound was forming on the ground a little bit in front of the juniper that Wan was perched on. She removed her head cam and placed it facing the ferrets. Now she could look around without annoying the rest of the team.

The crumbly dirt of the mound collapsed, revealing a tunnel. A tan, furry head peeked into view from the depths. The critter saw Wangari and swiftly ducked back, then reemerged more cautiously, its dark eyes pleading up at her.

She was able to glimpse that it was hugging something close to its fat chest, absently fidgeting with it. The angle was bad and the animal stuck to the shadows, but she thought it looked like a metal teacup. Maybe somebody had dropped it and the scruffy prairie dog had hoarded it for himself, allured by its shiny silver glimmer.

Cute, she thought.

"Hey, man, is it true? They're releasing *ferrets*? Here? Today? FERRETS?"

In spite of the fact that it seemed bigger and more well fed than the prairie dogs back at the Ark, this specimen had clearly had a tough life. Its shadowy face had several old scars, and the head looked a little deformed. A drab tan in color, it nervously kept to the dark of its tunnel, never really poking out.

"They are indeed releasing ferrets," Wan told it. "Hobbs and Jill, down there in that cage, are moving in."

The creature's accent was thick, and it spoke quickly in a low whisper. "Grab them and get out of here, man," it chittered. "Prairie dogs got enough problems with the hawks and the eagles and the coyotes and foxes. And a yahoo, hat-wearin' type that's always fussing and forcing us to act!"

"I feel you." Wangari nodded in solidarity. "Are you talking about Murray Sheridan?"

"Yes! Him! We're taking heavy fire on all sides! We built these tunnels. . . . This land is ours." He yipped. It was a horrible-sounding yip, like hearing a fox try to meow, but in the distance, numerous prairie dogs yipped back.

"Yip! Yip!"

"You'll be fine," the pangolin reassured him. "Looks like you've survived a lot already. You have a name?"

"They call me Quag," answered the anxious critter, his beady eyes flitting about, this way and that. "But you can call me Quag." Dirt from the mound above him trickled down on his head. "You're not like other animals, are you?" Quag accused suspiciously.

"No, I'm not," Wangari agreed. She was very fond of her hyperintelligence, truth be told. She loved creating gadgets and doing acrobatics. "I sort of have an extrasmart brain."

"Well, aren't you fancy?" Quag disappeared down his hole.

Must be difficult at the bottom of the food web, Wangari thought sympathetically. She grabbed her head cam and put it back on as Dr. Fellows moved toward the ferret cage.

"Arief, do you copy?"

"I'm here," said the ape. "You were distracted by something?"

"I just got a visit from one of the locals," Wan reported. "Seems that the prairie dogs are aware the ferrets are moving in. And they know about Murray Sheridan. They don't like him."

"Hey, Wan?" said Murdock, his voice on edge. "Are you seeing what I'm seeing? Is the ground moving over by the cage?"

"Hold on," Wangari said. She put the binocs to her

eyes. The terrain over at the reintro site seemed to be . . . *bubbling.* "Weird," she remarked.

"It's not right. Something's happening," Arief warned. "Get closer, Wan. Check it out."

Wan jumped from the tree and dive-rolled to the ground. Her heart rate increased. She picked herself up, clipped the binocs to her harness, and hurried on her hind legs down the hillside, keeping out of sight by angling toward the parked vehicles.

But by the time she got closer, it was too late: a swarm of prairie dogs, a thousand strong, erupted from the ground along the meadow's far slope.

The rodents boiled up everywhere. Wan leaped out of the way to avoid falling into a hole. The critters burst forth and stampeded over the surface of the pasture, overwhelming Wan. She couldn't get to Hobbs and Jill. Her view of the humans and the cage was blocked by the jeep.

The prairie dogs turned on her—and then attacked. Their coordination was amazing. They seemed to swarm with one mind, like a school of fish. They swirled around Wan, corralling her, no matter how much she tried to dance away.

All right, let's switch this up a bit.

She threw herself downhill and curled into a ball, her armored plates stiff and locked. She rolled down the slope, but her assailants kept pace. They stopped her forward momentum and prairie dog–piled her where she lay.

"Okay. Plan C, then." Within her tight huddle, she uncurled enough to access the smoke canister in her harness. She lit it with the butane torch Velcroed into her left shoulder strap and tossed the device out.

The fuse sparkled and made the canister spin. It released dark, black smoke in a spiraling stream. The attackers backed away, coughing.

Wangari seized the moment. Goggles lowered, breath held, she locked her eyes on the cargo rack at the top of Dr. Fellows's jeep, which was just visible through the gathering black mist. She shot her sucker launcher at it, and it connected beautifully. Wan engaged the motor reel and was instantly whipped forward and upward, away from her attackers.

She slammed into the back of the jeep hard and was dragged upward to where she could grab the cargo rack and pull herself to safety.

"Are you okay?" Arief asked in a panic.

"Affirmative, I'm alive and out of the way," Wan

reported brusquely, catching her breath and detaching the sucker cup from the jeep. She tucked the device back into place on her harness.

"What about the ferrets?" the orangutan demanded.

Wan gathered her bearings. She stood up on the jeep, looking back at the hill she had just crossed. The prairie dogs were vanishing back into their holes, yipping and whooping.

Answering waves of yips rose throughout the colony.

"Yip! Yip!"

Wan turned to face forward and dropped quickly to her stomach when she saw Dr. Fellows and Officer Nez.

"Where are Jill and Hobbs?" Arief insisted.

"I don't see them," Wan said. "Just a sec."

She scrambled forward on the roof of the jeep. The reintroduction site came into full view. The two humans were holding their heads, gasping in disbelief. The prairie dogs had vanished. The meadow was quiet and still. The table was flipped over, and next to it, the ferret cage lay on its side, its door swung wide open.

Wangari scanned the pasture several times, with no results.

Hobbs and Jill were gone.

CHAPTER EIGHTEEN

ARIEF

(Pongo abelii)

Back at headquarters, Arief paced.

If we had left when I originally wanted to, we would have been there in time to stop this.

The great ape couldn't stay still. He watched the monitors. He went in and out of the tilt-rotor, inventorying supplies. He shouted orders at Murdock, who was already hurrying things along as fast as he could.

Wangari was making her fourth or fifth sweep of the reintroduction site, or maybe even her sixth—Arief was losing track. The pangolin had ducked her head into countless burrows. Nothing: no sign of the ferrets anywhere.

The situation was hopeless. Arief was powerless to do anything about it, other than watch. He thumped his chest in frustration and returned once more to the cockpit of *Red Tail*.

The black tilt-rotor aircraft with the red stripe on the fin, emblazoned along the hull with the Endangereds insignia, was loaded with supplies. It was pointed toward the Big Top's sealed bay door. Murdock's plan to keep the Ark's poo-bot army happy during Arief's and Wan's absences was already in motion, with the assistance of new programming code directing the jungle hab Poop-E to report directly to the narwhal at collection times.

Arief finished another pointless inspection of the craft and knuckled back over to the monitors.

He was still baffled by what had gone down. It was pretty clear from what little footage Wan could collect from her viewpoint that Jill and Hobbs had unexpectedly vanished. The frantic conversations going on between the humans seemed to confirm that. Dr. Fellows and Officer Nez were also confused and had no real answers, which suggested to Arief the truth was as outrageous as it appeared to be: the ferrets had been taken away against their will.

But that was absurd. Prairie dogs weren't smart enough to organize a rodent uprising. Something else, or someone else, was behind this.

"I saw tears of frustration at one point," Wan reported. "They have no idea what happened. Fellows is preparing to head back to the ranger station."

"Stay on them," Arief ordered. "I'm leaving as soon as Murdock finishes uploading the autopilot configurations. We'll do our own sweep of the site first thing in the morning. Meanwhile, you keep an eye on the rangers so we know what their next move is."

"Copy," Wan said. "I think they're out of ideas, though."

Arief watched the big screens as Wangari stealthily darted toward Dr. Fellows's jeep.

He was exhausted by it all. He rested his head on his crossed arms at the desk. He felt light-headed and weak. *I should have insisted on monitoring the release in person.*

"Why did I let that polar bear overrule me?" he asked the empty room. "She's not even a part of this." He hissed with regret.

Nukilik hadn't been in the Big Top for the reintroduction live feed. She hadn't witnessed any of the craziness. She'd been up all night conducting her own search for her home and was catching up on sleep.

Fine with me, Arief had concluded. *She's useless, anyway.*

Murdock appeared at the pool with an update. "I was just over at the tank to upload the course I plotted. I saw Nuk and explained to her what just went down."

"And?" Arief asked pointedly.

The narwhal shrugged using his tiny flippers. "She listened, but she didn't say much. I'm not sure she understands how serious the situation is."

"So much for hoping she would come around." Arief sighed.

"Anyway, you're all set. Once I decompress the chamber and open the bay door, you're clear to go."

"Thank you, Murdock. Sorry I've been so short tempered."

Murdock waved him off. "Every second counts. I just wish I could figure out a way to join you. Next time . . . with the exo-suit."

Wan's voice chimed in through the speakers. She

was holding her head cam in her paw as she clung to the back of the jeep, heading away from the reintro site along a bumpy dirt road.

"Hey, Arief," the pangolin said, her voice wavering as the vehicle jostled. "I've been thinking. While you're on your way, I should use the time to do some recon on this Murray Sheridan dude. I've got a bad feeling about him. I wonder if he was somehow involved. I have time, and it's the only lead I can think of."

Arief shrugged. "Good idea. We need all the intel we can get."

"When I get to the station," Wan suggested, "I'll find Sheridan's address and head over there on foot. Maybe it'll be a dead end. But we'll cross him off the list as a suspect, at least."

"Do it," said Arief. "Just find out what the rangers are planning before you take off."

Arief marched back over to the cockpit and sat himself down at the helm. He adjusted a few dials and made sure the seat belts and headset fit comfortably. His stomach filled with a familiar worry. The tilt-rotor essentially flew itself, but there was always a risk to leaving the ground and taking off at high speeds. And when he was honest with himself, he wished Murdock could come with him. He hated having to go alone.

Arief glanced out of the open cabin door and gave Murdock a wave. The narwhal nodded his tusk. "Give me a minute to reach my command center, and I'll open the bay door."

Just as the narwhal vanished, Nukilik ran into the Big Top.

Arief sighed. *Right back to searching coastlines?*

But the polar bear passed by the computer terminals and approached *Red Tail.* She strode up the ramp, gnawing her bone, something black draped over her shoulder.

She crouched in the tilt-rotor's doorway, soaking in the view. The cockpit was large and open, with ample room to spare even with a polar bear inside. "When did you learn how to fly this thing?" she asked Arief.

"It pretty much flies itself," Arief answered. "I can show you when I get back."

"I found my home," the polar bear said.

"You did?"

Nuk nodded. "I think so. I'm pretty sure I've got the spot nailed down."

Arief was quiet for a moment. He arched an eyebrow.

"We don't have the fuel to do everything in one trip."

"I know," said Nukilik.

Arief paused, about to say something, when he was interrupted by Murdock on the comm. "Okay. Coast is clear. Big Top is depressurized. Opening doors now. You're a go for launch."

"Hobbs and Jill—are they going to be okay?" Nukilik asked.

The great ape shook his head. "I don't know. They vanished."

"What about you?" she pressed. "Can you do this mission by yourself?"

"I've got Murdock. And Wan is on-site," Arief pointed out, not really answering the question.

Nukilik just stood there, examining the interior of the craft.

Arief gestured for her to get off the ramp, then he flipped a few levers and punched the ignition. The onboard displays flickered to life. The propellers along the wings, currently in airplane mode, started spinning and gathering speed. *Red Tail* lurched forward. Still standing on the ramp, Nukilik jerked, holding herself steady by grabbing the door's frame.

"I have to lift the ramp," Arief called over to her. "In or out?"

Surprisingly, Nukilik stepped forward. She took the object flung over her shoulder and awkwardly slipped her arms through its holes. It turned out to be a protective vest marked with the Endangereds logo. "I can't let you do this alone," she shouted over the gathering noise. "Sorry, but I'm coming."

"Fine. Then strap in," Arief said, keeping his tone neutral. "Welcome aboard."

The Big Top's curved wall slid open, and *Red Tail* rolled out into the night onto a gravelly lot with no runway. The wing propellers rotated upward, and the plane/helicopter shot into the air.

Nukilik had taken a seat just in time. She yelped in surprise as they quickly rose over the Pacific Ocean.

Arief smiled and whispered to himself, "I love it when a plan comes together."

CHAPTER NINETEEN

WANGARI

(Phataginus tetradactyla)

Wangari caught her breath, looking toward a ramshackle old house nestled against a nook in the hill. A flatbed trailer stacked with plywood was parked beside it.

She shed her harness weighed down with gear and rolled her neck. She tapped her headset and adjusted her mic, which had jiggled askew during her long gallop here. "I'm going in for a closer look."

She lowered her brass goggles over her eyes, careful not to jostle the camera, and scampered forward. Her legs were tired. The sun was low on the horizon now, but she had made it to Murray Sheridan's farm with a little daylight to spare.

Dr. Fellows and the ranger had spent most of the afternoon on the phone, and at their computers. Their concern seemed genuine to Wan. But the plan they had developed wasn't good enough. They were going to monitor the reintroduction site for several weeks, placing live traps and motion cameras throughout the immediate area. If the ferrets managed to get themselves captured or photographed, the team would then discuss next steps.

What the wildlife managers hadn't said out loud was what failure would mean for the prairie dog colony. Without natural predators around, the managers would have to do something to keep the prairie dog population in control. That might mean allowing humans to hunt them.

The truth was: more prairie dogs would die *without* the ferrets in place.

And that would be more than a simple tragedy. The Gunnison's prairie dog was a keystone species in this type of sagebrush ecosystem. Prairie dogs kept soil and plant communities healthy and provided food for lots of animal species. Their abandoned burrows became homes for ferrets but also for other weasels, burrowing owls, badgers, snakes, foxes, and countless insects.

The more Wan thought about it, the clearer it became: it was critical for the Endangereds to help Hobbs and Jill and their kits succeed out here. This was what the Endangereds were all about, in the end: bringing balance back to nature, which meant working to protect the entire food web.

Of course, for any of this to pan out, we need to find Hobbs and Jill alive.

Wan's earpiece crackled to life. "Hey, Wan? Do you see those?"

Arief's voice shook Wan out of her thoughts. She gazed straight ahead and saw the plywood boards in Sheridan's trailer bed. They were cut out in the shapes of prairie dogs. Red targets were spray-painted on them, and they were riddled with paintball blotches.

"Freeze on the license plate," Murdock suggested. "I'll run a background check."

Wangari did as the narwhal asked, and Murdock came back with some interesting results a moment later.

"I would definitely follow up on this," he advised the pangolin. "This guy has a rap sheet as long as my tusk."

"I figured as much. That's why I'm here," said Wan.

"Well, that's odd," mentioned the narwhal back in the Galápagos. "Looks like the list of complaints . . . they were filed *by* Sheridan—*against* local law enforcement."

"He seems pretty worked up about things," said Arief from the cockpit of *Red Tail*, which was currently flying somewhere over Mexico.

Nukilik added, "Maybe you should get out of there, Wan."

"Not yet. I'm missing something here; I can feel it. I'm going in."

"Be careful," Arief insisted.

"Imagine if this guy sees an African black-bellied pangolin walking around his property with a camera strapped to its noggin," Murdock said. "Conspiracy much?"

After a short sprint and a big leap, Wan landed on the railing of the cabin porch. She yelped in alarm. A large jackrabbit sat upright on a rocking chair, staring out upon the sage-covered hills. Its ears pointed straight up, as if on full alert.

It was dead, Wan realized. Stuffed. The rabbit's large marble eyes peered blankly out at the range.

Wan leaped over to the porch window. The glass was smear-streaked with dirt and draped on the inside with a thin brown curtain. She couldn't make out anything within other than vague shapes of furniture.

"I don't see or hear anyone inside," the pangolin reported. "I'm going in."

She scrambled to the side of the house and found a cracked-open window. *Perfect infiltration point.* With a running start, she clawed her way up the wall and hooked into the windowsill. She pulled herself up, raised the window, and dropped into the cabin interior.

Wan lifted her goggles and took a look around.

The surfaces were messily strewn with discarded junk. The stuffed head of a deer jutted out from the wall over a saggy, green couch. The buck's antlers branched out and hovered over the room, a checkered shirt dangling from one of the points. A hawk was poised on a perch, frozen in the act of launching for flight. A fox crouched in midprowl from atop an end table.

"Wan, seriously, you should hightail it," the narwhal advised. "I'm getting bad vibes here."

"I hear you," Wan said. "Just give me another minute." And that's when she noticed a weird-looking, bulky backpack with various hoses. She crawled closer. It was labeled on the sides in big red letters with:

U-SUCK!® VAC-U-PAK®
D.I.Y. HUMANE RODENT REMOVAL™

The E at the end of the word "Humane" had mostly faded off. There was a picture of a happy mouse waving from inside the collection chamber of a household vacuum cleaner. Beneath the cartoonish drawing was the italicized caption:

VAC-U-PAK®:
WHEN LIFE BLOWS, U-SUCK!®™

"What the heck is all this about?" Wan asked everyone. "He's catching them alive?"

"Wan, I just saw a light sweeping across the wall," Arief observed. "You sure you're alone?"

Right then the pangolin heard tires crackling on the dirt road outside.

"Not anymore, from the sound of it."

An engine grew steadily louder. Headlights shone through the curtained windows. There was no mistaking it: a vehicle was coming up the driveway, fast.

CHAPTER TWENTY

WANGARI

(Phataginus tetradactyla)

"Time to go, Wan!" Arief insisted.

"No. Not yet."

"You're ignoring a direct order," the orangutan growled.

"We're not done here," Wan shot back. "Let me scan the place. You can do a more careful review of the footage once I'm out."

"Fine. Just make it quick."

"I thought I caught a glimpse of a notebook and some documents piled on the kitchen counter," Nukilik gruffly mentioned. "Can you get a closer look at them?"

"Copy that." The pangolin sprang onto the table and knocked over an empty copper cup. She winced: it clanged loudly when it fell. She hopped across the gap onto the counter and ambled over to a mess of papers.

"Stop there for a sec," asked the polar bear.

Wangari let her camera linger on the open notebook, which had a detailed pencil sketch of a ferret. It was a pretty good drawing. She flipped the page, finding drawings of other animals, including prairie dogs.

She turned the page again—and gasped.

"What is that a drawing of?" Arief asked right away.

"I'm not sure what it is," Wan confessed, turning the sketch in different directions, "but I saw one of the prairie dogs carrying something like this just before the chaos started." The drawing looked like it could be some kind of metallic cup or bowl with some basic electronic componentry fused to it.

"'And Bingo was his name-o,'" Murdock guessed. "Those capacitors on the side can send and receive electromagnetic signals. I have a hunch what it's for. Can you check the other rooms for any weird radio equipment?"

"What will it look like?" Wan asked.

"I'll know it when I see it."

"You might even find the ferrets," Nukilik surmised.

"Just be quick!" Arief urged.

Wan looked toward the cabin's dark hallway, but stopped short, her eyes snagged on another loose paper sitting on the table. She hopped over to study it.

"Some sort of map," Nukilik noted.

"Could these be prairie dog tunnels?" Wan wondered aloud, following a dizzying array of forking paths, each branch narrower than the one before.

"In my expert opinion as a digging animal," quipped Murdock, "definitely."

"That settles it," Arief murmured. "This guy had some role in whatever happened."

Outside the cabin, Wan heard a truck door open and close.

"I don't think I have time to explore the other rooms," she said, glancing toward the kitchen window.

"We've seen enough," Arief agreed. "Get out of there."

Wan jumped off the table and crept over beneath the high window, positioning herself at the ready. She could hear the human struggling to lift something out of the back of the truck. Then footsteps crackled nearer, finally reaching the wooden planks of the porch.

Now. Wangari leaped. Her powerful claws gripped the sill, but the old wood pulled away from the wall and she crashed back down to the floor.

The doorknob rattled. Wan righted herself and jumped onto the nearby end table. She crouched behind the stiff hawk on display there, held her breath, and stayed as still as she could.

The door swung open. Wan didn't move a muscle, frozen like the stuffed animals surrounding her.

"That's him," Murdock confirmed. "Murray Sheridan. Watch yourself, Wan."

Wangari didn't dare breathe.

From the door, Mr. Sheridan took off his cowboy hat and flung it straight at the pangolin.

It looped over the stuffed hawk's head and stayed there. Right behind the hawk, Wangari flinched only the slightest bit and gulped back a cry of alarm.

"Still got the touch," the man crowed.

The hat blocked Wan's view of Sheridan and the rest of the room. But she resisted the urge to lean around the obstacle.

Sheridan groaned, stretched, and shuffled to the kitchen, where the pangolin had a better angle to watch him. After clanging around in a cupboard for a copper cup and a glass bottle, he poured himself a drink and strode back out onto the porch.

"Now!" barked Nukilik. "Go!"

Wangari eyed the window longingly but shook her head. "I can't make it out that way," she whispered. "There's nothing firm to grip anymore." She peeked around the hat toward the porch. The front door was open, but Sheridan had settled into the rocking chair beside the jackrabbit.

He lifted his copper cup to the petrified hare. "Cheers, Jack. How's your rheumatism? Reckon the monsoons'll be early?"

Wangari hopped to the floor and dashed toward the open door. Her heart quickened. A couple strides and a leap off the porch steps and she could scurry away before Sheridan could react. She just needed for him to look away for a second.

"Jack! No, no, no. You see that!" Sheridan grew suddenly agitated, abruptly coming to attention in his rocking chair. "Back already? I told you I've had enough!

What's it gonna take?"

Framed in the doorway, far off among the sage-brush, the pangolin saw a mound of moist, crumbly dirt forming. A few seconds later, the head of a prairie dog appeared. Wan did a double take—if she didn't know any better, she might have sworn the little critter wore a taunting smile.

Is that Quag? Wan wasn't sure. She wished she had the binoculars handy, but she had ditched her heavier gear in the bunch grasses outside. The critter in the distance shared the same dented head that she had noticed from before, but it was far away and the sky was growing dark.

Sheridan lost his cool. He sprang out of his chair and threw his copper cup toward the prairie dog. "I've had it with all of you! Why won't you listen to me? You're out of your furry, rotten minds, all of you!"

The mischievous creature yipped joyously in return. An answering chatter, as if in laughter, called out from other unseen prairie dogs.

"Yip! Yip!"

"That's it!" Sheridan pivoted on the porch. "I'm

grabbing my U-Suck!" He stormed inside and reached for the strange backpack beside the door.

And that's when Sheridan saw Wan.

The two locked eyes. "What the devil kind of armadillo are you?"

The man's gaze absorbed the camera and earpiece strapped to Wan's head. Sheridan gasped. He pointed. "I knew it! You're working with them, aren't you?"

He lofted the backpack at her.

The pangolin ducked and made her move toward the door. But the backpack connected. It was surprisingly heavy.

Wangari fell flat against the wooden floor, out cold.

CHAPTER TWENTY-ONE

ARIEF

(Pongo abelii)

The tilt-rotor video screens went suddenly dark.

Somewhere high above Mexico, traveling north at nearly four hundred miles an hour, Arief felt his heart flip. He accelerated the aircraft. Flying at max speed would use up more fuel, but he didn't care.

"No!" Nukilik barked, rattling the dead screen. "Get it back! Do something!"

Arief nudged her. "Nuk, you're going to break it." He gripped his hands into fists. "This is what happens when no one listens to me!"

But then, like magic, the dashboard monitors flickered back to life.

"Thank the figs." Arief sighed. But his celebration was short lived.

Front and center on the screen was Murray Sheridan close-up, his nostrils flaring, as he inspected Wangari's tiny camera unit pinched in his fingers. The Endangereds watched with bated breath for any sign of Wangari as the view shifted back and forth.

"Who's on the other end of this thing?" Sheridan wondered aloud, frowning with suspicion. "Are you watching me now? Huh? WHO ARE YOU?"

The Endangereds were silent as they studied the feed. They cut off their mics, just to be safe.

"There! Look!" Arief exclaimed, pointing toward a bulky object on the floor of the cabin that was visible as the image spun.

"Rewind it," Nukilik said.

The orangutan got to work on a secondary monitor and slowed the playback down. The object was definitely armored, like Wangari. "That's her. Look, she's moving!"

"I knew she was tough." Nukilik grunted with relief.

They toggled back to the live feed. "He'd better watch out," Murdock noted with a gurgle. "If he doesn't wise up real soon, he's about to— Yup."

Sheridan cried out, and the camera jostled violently. They caught another glimpse of Wangari, at Sheridan's feet, spinning like a top and lashing her tail at the guy's boots. He lost his footing and spilled to the ground. Wan jabbed her micro-Taser into his side and discharged it. Sheridan yowled in pain and tossed the camera away.

"Get out of there!" the remote team shouted at the video screens.

Wan high-scaled it for the exit. Her large fore claws latched on to the headset device, and then the image swung, showing only the pangolin's feet as Wangari hopped once, twice, and then shot out the front door of the cabin as a whirling ball. She hit the ground on her feet and sprinted into the brush.

A minute later, *Red Tail*'s dash binged. A pleasant, automated voice announced, "Estimated time of arrival: three hours."

"Come in, *Red Tail*, Big Top," rang the pangolin's voice after another few minutes. Wangari's headset was back in place. The screen showed her viewpoint: perched on a boulder looking out at a rocky terrain from the edge of a plateau. The western horizon blazed a burnt orange. The cabin looked small against the vast landscape. Wan was panting heavily. "Do you read?"

Arief switched their audio back on. "We saw the whole thing," he told her. "Are you safe?"

"I'm okay," she said. "I don't think he's coming after me."

"We'll arrive before midnight," said Arief. "I need you to scope out a place we can land."

"I've got just the spot." She turned 180 degrees, framing the screen on the next rise in the hills where there was a sandy wash lined with cottonwood trees. The image was dim and grainy. Wan pointed in that direction. "I'll head over there. I'm sure it has clearings in the trees that'll hide *Red Tail*."

"Just send us the coordinates when you have them," said Arief. "And don't go back to the cabin without us."

"But I didn't explore the whole house. I want to confirm if there's broadcasting equipment. And the ferrets might even be there, held captive somewhere."

"You need backup. Get some rest. We'll plan a

predawn operation together once we're on the ground. That's an order, Wan."

"Copy that." The pangolin sighed. "Over and out." The screen image was replaced with a virtual dashboard, showing dials and settings and flight information panels.

"Why don't we land right on top of that house?" Nukilik grunted. "Smash it to bits. We need to take that crazy guy out!" She bit down on her bone as if to drive home her point.

"No, Nuk!" Arief shot back. "We still don't have the full picture. We need a plan. And we're not going to injure any humans, or harm their property, if we can help it. No aggression. We fight only in self-defense.

"Wouldn't it be easier to just alert the authorities?" Murdock asked over the comm. "Serious question. We could edit some footage together, take some screen grabs, email the people in charge—"

"No," Arief answered firmly. "We can't solve this by passing the problem on to others. Murray Sheridan has a long history of making trouble. The humans already knew about him, but they never acted. Now it's up to us to get Hobbs and Jill back."

This far south, and at their altitude, the sun was just now setting. They were passing over a mountainous part of northern Mexico.

"So, what do you have in mind?" Nukilik asked.

"Sheridan already knows about Wan," Arief started. "He's a loner. He's been causing trouble for a while. If we can't gather enough intel on our own, we may have to risk something more . . . drastic. . . ." The ape trailed off, hesitant to voice his radical proposal out loud. It was extreme, especially in light of what he'd just said to Nuk about doing as little harm as possible, but there might be no other way. "I want to be prepared, just in case we have to go big."

"I don't get it. What are you driving at?" Nukilik asked.

Arief spit it out: "We may need to kidnap the kidnapper."

CHAPTER TWENTY-TWO

NUKILIK

(Ursus maritimus)

Nukilik crouched behind the white septic tank beside Sheridan's cabin. When she had learned what the tank's purpose was, she had balked, but she was resigned to the fact that it was the most natural camouflage she was going to get in these parts.

Using binoculars, she scanned the porch and the windows for signs of movement within the home. It was still dark, but morning was on the way, and visibility was improving with every minute. Things appeared still for once. Maybe Sheridan had finally stopped pacing and gone to sleep.

"We're running out of cover," Wangari reminded everyone. "Once the sun rises, *Red Tail* will be visible for miles in every direction. It's now or never."

"He may have finally gone to bed," Nukilik reported.

We could have just done this when he was wide awake, Nuk thought again. But the others had trusted Arief's reasoning for waiting so long.

She turned her head and glanced high and to the north, where she could just make out the tilt-rotor hovering in position several thousand feet up. She stole a glimpse at it with the binocs. Wangari was up there, manually piloting the craft in hover mode. A long rope ladder hung from its belly like a spider's thread.

Arief was on his mark in the shadows of the cabin porch, locked and loaded.

Nukilik was positioned for close-up surveillance. If things went south, they wanted some muscle on the ground. Otherwise, Nukilik had been strictly instructed to hang back and keep an extremely low profile. Not a natural feat for a polar bear. Crouching like this was putting a real crick in her neck.

She might have protested more, but the truth was she didn't mind playing a supporting role. All this snooping around was nerve-racking.

Originally, Arief had hoped Wangari could sneak back inside the house during the night, search the remaining rooms of the cabin, and report back to the group. But no such luck: Sheridan had remained awake all night long.

"This is what I feared," Arief had finally decided. "Let's fall back."

And so they had switched up the plan: kidnap Sheridan and *then* search the house.

"Why all the caution?" Nukilik had wondered. "I could just barrel in there, knock him flat."

"He may have a gun," Arief had explained. "I don't want anyone hurt."

So many extra parts to this plan, she thought to herself.

But Nukilik didn't argue, which left the big mammals on the ground to overwhelm Sheridan while Wan was airborne nearby, hover-parked in the getaway vehicle.

Nukilik needed to relax. She rolled her shoulder to

help release the tension. "Argh," she grouched. "Neck's killing me."

"No kidding?" Murdock chuckled from half a world away. He suddenly spoke with a thick English accent, narrating: "Burrowed in the dirt behind a capsule full of sewage, deep in the wild frontier of the American southwest, the giant polar bear basks in her natural habitat." He switched back to his normal voice. "Can't imagine why you've got a crick in your spine."

"Cut the chatter," Nukilik complained. She was in no mood for jokes. She was really on edge.

"He's related to dolphins." Arief grunted. "Chattering's all he's good for."

"You're a regular standing-up comedian, aren't you, Arief?" Murdock spouted. "Keep throwing us zingers."

"I'd think twice before asking an ape to throw stuff at you," advised the pangolin.

"All right!" barked the orangutan. "Nuk's right: time to focus. I'm ready to knock now."

Nukilik watched as Arief carefully ascended the steps. "Wan, redeploy to your mark. When Murray comes to the door, he should be groggy and off guard, but everyone be ready for anything."

The polar bear tensed. "Copy that. Standing by." She found herself nervous but excited, ready for action but also uncertain.

The orangutan knocked on the door.

Nukilik could hear the tilt-rotor drawing closer quickly.

"Who is it!" Sheridan shouted angrily.

Arief pounded on the door again.

"All right! I'm coming! I'm coming!"

Heavy footsteps marched through the house.

Murray Sheridan threw open the front door, head to toe in white long johns.

Murdock offered a low chuckle. "Orangutan. Orangutan who?"

A deafening explosion ripped through the air. Instantly, Murray Sheridan went flying to the ground, tangled up in a great weave of big-game netting. At the other end of the porch, smoke rose out of the barrel of Arief's net launcher.

Murdock crowed. "Orangutan on safari! That's who."

A suspicious stillness came over the cabin. Sheridan moaned on the ground, balled up and pinned down, squirming but dazed.

The great ape tossed his spent tool to the floorboards. "That about wraps things up," he grunted.

Nukilik sprang forward on shaky legs. She lit a flare and waved it at the approaching tilt-rotor. Wangari guided *Red Tail* into position over the cabin. The slack end of the rope ladder bunched up on the porch steps.

Arief attached Sheridan's net to the ladder using the prongs of a grappling hook. He glanced at the tangled-up human then up at the aircraft. "I've bagged my limit for the day, Wan."

Wangari saluted from the cockpit. "I'm inbound," Nuk heard her say over the radio. "Murdock, you have the controls."

"Affirmative," the narwhal confirmed.

Nukilik looked skyward. Her eyes widened at the tilt-rotor high overhead. A spread-eagle pangolin, wearing goggles and a backpack—a parachute guideline trailing behind her—plummeted toward the earth.

Great green ribbons. The polar bear gritted her teeth. *Now she's just showing off.*

"Nukilik, let's go!" Arief called out over the noise of the hovering aircraft.

She galloped over to the steps and reached out to

grab the rising rope ladder just in time. While it took all her strength simply to hold on, spinning in circles right below Sheridan's tangled mass, Arief had already climbed halfway up the ladder's length.

Several hundred feet high in the air over the desert Southwest, the orangutan looked perfectly at ease.

Red Tail banked left toward its landing site half a mile away along the dry creek bed. With the first rays of the sun now hitting the hills in the distance, Nukilik watched Wangari deploy her red, green, and yellow parachute. Wangari landed hard on the cabin roof, rolling into a ball to absorb the blow. She detached the chute with a fluid motion and swung off the gutter onto the porch.

With the cabin to herself, she'd make quick work of finding the ferrets, or at least getting more answers.

Nukilik had to admit: Arief's plan had worked in the end. *Lucky ape*, she muttered to herself.

For a second she could see it all coming together: they would rescue the ferrets quickly, head home to refuel, and then . . . finally, she could go home and find her mother. *She'll never believe where I've been and what I've done!*

"Orange leader, come in."

"Go ahead, Wan. What'd you find?"

"That's just it." She grunted in frustration over the radio. "Nothing. No ferrets. No broadcasting equipment. No weird devices. The bedrooms are empty. There's no basement. No guns. No cages. There's literally nothing of note here that we haven't already seen."

CHAPTER TWENTY-THREE

ARIEF

(Pongo abelii)

Arief hopped out of *Red Tail* and made his way toward Nukilik. He couldn't believe what Wan had just announced. How was there no connection between Sheridan and their missing friends? If Sheridan wasn't somehow involved in the ferrets' disappearance, then who was?

"This isn't adding up," he said under his breath.

"So much for the best-laid schemes of mice and . . . other mammals," Murdock grumbled from his post in the Galápagos.

"It's not funny, Murdock," Arief growled. "We're back to square one."

"What in the devil is a *polar bear* doing here?" Murray Sheridan bellowed.

Nuk gave the human a menacing growl.

Sheridan writhed in the net, trying to get free. "I knew this day was coming. I knew you were an organized bunch. I tried to warn everyone, but no one listened!"

Arief came between Sheridan and Nuk. "We're only here to protect the ferrets," he said, letting his own short temper show. "If you have them, hand them back!"

"Ferrets?" the man protested. "What ferrets? What do ferrets have to do with it? And protect them from what? Me? I'm not a threat. *They're* the maniacs!"

"What are you talking about?" Arief asked. "Who's *they*?"

"Them!" shouted Sheridan. His hands were tangled in the netting so he pointed with his chin.

Arief frowned.

Sheridan wasn't nearly as surprised to be arguing with a talking orangutan and a polar bear as he should have been.

What am I missing? Arief asked himself.

Then he remembered what Sheridan had said while the pangolin was recording him last evening:

"I've had it with all of you! Why won't you listen to me? You're out of your furry, rotten minds!"

And just a moment ago:

"I knew you were an organized bunch. I tried to warn everyone, but no one listened!"

Arief groaned.

"What is it?" Nuk asked him.

The great ape stood over Sheridan and tried to help him sit up within the netting. The man flinched and shrank away. "Take your stinking paws off me, you dang dirty ape!"

Arief ignored the insult. "You've seen other animals act weird, haven't you?"

Sheridan nodded but didn't elaborate.

"But you're not behind it."

Sheridan nodded again.

"And you were never arguing against the ferret release, were you? You were complaining about—"

"The prairie dogs!" Sheridan sneered. "Yes. Finally! Someone gets it!"

Arief slapped a palm on his head. "Sheridan's not the bad guy," he said.

"Then who is?" demanded Murdock in his ears.

Arief searched his thoughts while rubbing his chin, conjuring up a word. "Hey, Wan," he asked, "tell me more about . . . what did you call him? Quag. Do you remember anything strange about him?"

"Uh . . ." Arief could hear jostling and rattling in the background as Wangari thought out loud. "I didn't get a good look." Her voice was choppy, for some reason. "He was pretty banged up. A bit chubby. Oh, and he was carrying that thing when I saw him. A cup, like the one Sheridan drew a picture of."

Arief turned to Sheridan. "In your house, on the counter, we saw a drawing of a metal cup that had some weird circuitry. Why'd you draw that? What is it, exactly?"

"Huh?" Sheridan said, but then he remembered. "Oh. I know what you're aiming at. You're talking about the alien artifact."

CHAPTER TWENTY-FOUR

NUKILIK

(Ursus maritimus)

Nukilik leaned in on Sheridan. "What did you say?"

"Aliens?" blurted Murdock excitedly in her ear. "Aliens!"

"What are aliens?" Nukilik asked, confused.

"Little green men!" Murdock gurgled, barely able to contain himself. "From outer space! They're, like, animals from other planets."

"From the stars?" asked Nukilik.

"That's not what we're dealing with here," scolded Arief. He turned to Nukilik with a grim expression, wanting to be perfectly clear.

"Why ain't it?" Sheridan challenged him, struggling to sit up. He was still entangled in the netting. "What else would it be? What else could make prairie dogs so organized?"

"Some kind of new tech, for sure," Arief allowed. "That doesn't mean it originates on another world. Did you *see* aliens?" he asked Sheridan.

"No. But I'm having a conversation with an ape and a polar bear right now, ain't I? So prove me wrong."

"He's got an interesting point," Murdock chimed in.

Arief seemed flummoxed. He stumbled over his words for a second before finding his verbal footing. "Let's stay focused here. We know something strange is going on, but we don't need to fixate on the most outlandish explanations."

"Fine," Sheridan huffed. "I agree. I don't care if that object is alien based or a top-secret government program or ancient Mayan technology—the prairie dogs have it, and they've been nothing but a nightmare since they got it. My crops are destroyed. I haven't had a harvest in two years. I've been meaning to buy some cattle but can't afford to now. They stole my golf cart and my furniture. So, riddle me that."

"Something very wrong is going on here," Arief repeated.

"But what are we going to *do*?" asked Nukilik.

"We need a plan," said Arief.

"Another plan!" Nuk snorted. "Always another plan!"

Just then Sheridan's truck came roaring over the hill, followed by a plume of dust. It caught some air on the rise, sailing ahead. Nuk could see Wangari driving, gripping the steering wheel. The truck landed hard, front wheels first, then back, then front again. Something flew out of the bed of the pickup.

"Hey, easy on the shocks, would ya?" Sheridan shouted.

The tires slid to a halt on the loose gravel of the road, twenty or thirty feet in front of *Red Tail*. Wan sprang from the door, fully geared up. A two-by-four toppled to the ground. Nuk guessed Wan had used it to reach the pedals.

"The armadillo's back!" Sheridan cried.

"I'm a *pangolin*! Come on!" Wangari shouted to her associates. "Forget the rancher. He doesn't know anything, and our friends are still missing. Time's wasting."

Something snapped in Nukilik. *Wangari's right!* "This is ridiculous," she declared. "We should be tunneling after the prairie dogs! The answers are clearly underground." She looked around, saw an old prairie dog burrow nearby, and started digging into it with her massive paws, kicking up shovelfuls of dirt.

Arief spoke up. "If we're going underground, we need to be smart. There could be miles of tunnels down there, and they're all only a few inches wide."

"Actually," Sheridan said, "in some places, they're wide enough to fit couches and golf carts and whatnot."

Nukilik stopped digging. "What?" she and Arief said together.

"I've been telling you!" Sheridan loosened himself from the netting enough to sit up straight. "They stole my stuff! It's being kept down there somewhere in the maze."

Nukilik shared a look with Arief. She suddenly remembered the map Sheridan had sketched out. "Do you know where the entrance is?" she asked him.

"Course I do! I've only been in a little ways—it's a death trap down there. But free me, and I'll show you."

Arief nodded with satisfaction. "Great. Let's make tracks."

Murray Sheridan slowly met the orangutan's eyes. "Hold on a sec. Before I take another step, I need to know who you all are," he demanded, turning to all three animals present. "Where'd y'all come from?"

"We're an unnaturally selected posse of red-listed species," Wan summarized.

"Huh?"

"I'll explain on the way. Will you help us?" Arief asked him.

"If you cross your heart and swear to destroy that alien contraption, I'll point you in the right direction."

"We will," the ape told Sheridan. "But we need something else from you too."

"What's that?"

"Help us rescue our ferret friends. And if we manage to get control of the situation around here, I want you to agree to let them stay on your land."

Murray Sheridan considered the request suspiciously for a moment then perked up. "Ferrets'll keep the rodents in check, right?"

The animals nodded.

"Fair 'nough, I suppose. I reckon you've got yourselves a deal."

CHAPTER TWENTY-FIVE

NUKILIK

(Ursus maritimus)

"Who's that other feller y'all keep talkin' to in your walkie-talkie headsets?" Sheridan asked.

"Thar I blow!" Murdock quipped in Nukilik's ear.

"His name is Murdock," Wangari said.

"What is he? Let me guess. Wait. I know it. You've got a manatee on your team, don't you?" He laughed hard at his own joke.

The Endangereds all shared a look. It seemed that none of them wanted to admit how close the rancher was to the truth.

"Fine. Don't tell me. I probably don't want to know."

"Tell him I like his pajamas," Murdock grumbled.

"Murdock is pleased to meet you," Arief said instead. "And no, he's not a manatee. But we'll just leave it at that."

Arief, Wan, and Sheridan hustled toward the rancher's truck and hopped in the cabin. Nukilik grunted, knowing that she would be forced to ride in the bed due to her size.

Sheridan rummaged through a dirty duffel in the back, pulling out clothes that he put on over his long johns. "There's a tarp bunched up in the tool chest," he told the polar bear, adjusting a heavy leather vest over a plaid shirt. "If someone else comes along, I'll honk and you hide under it."

Sheridan drove off, navigating a network of empty dirt roads. It took them only a few minutes to arrive at an abandoned building. Part of the roof was collapsed. The stone foundation sagged in places, and the rock chimney had mostly crumbled away. The remains of an old fence enclosed a large hole in the ground.

They parked and jumped out of the truck. Nukilik adjusted her thick leather vest and fished a flashlight from one of the pockets.

"This property belonged to my family," Sheridan explained. "Hasn't been in use for decades—not by humans, leastways. But the root cellar there—goes down and down like an old mine shaft. You'll see."

He fished a large backpack out of the truck's cab and hoisted it awkwardly onto his shoulders, then strapped it into place. Nukilik recognized it instantly. It was the U-Suck!® Vac-U-Pak® device. The mouse waving from inside a vacuum cleaner's chamber looked happier than ever. Nukilik shook her head while reading the slogan: "Vac-U-Pak®: When life blows, U-Suck!®™" She wondered if her reading skills had gotten worse since leaving the Ark. The motto made no sense to her.

"Please tell me that's not a proton pack," joked Murdock, cracking himself up. "Remind him not to cross the streams."

"What are you going to do with that?" Arief asked the rancher.

"This ol' thing?" Sheridan hefted it into position with a proud smile. "This was designed for sewer workers in New York. City employees can suck up rats with it without hurting them. I ordered me one and made a few modifications. This'll make the vermin down there think twice."

The team descended into the root cellar. A cloud of dust kicked up when one of the old wooden steps snapped under Nukilik's weight, but she quickly steadied herself. Sheridan pulled away a tall square of rusty aluminum siding, exposing a hole that stretched into the earth.

Wan had a new gadget she'd fished out of *Red Tail*'s supplies: a pair of night vision goggles. She fitted them into place and flipped them on. Her eyes glowed green.

Nukilik gulped. She peered down into the black tunnel then stared at her tiny flashlight. Everything in her nature warned her not to proceed. She had explored ice caves and crevasses a few times in her life. She'd even followed her mother into an underwater cavity in an iceberg once. But those closed spaces were always lit by the sunlight that refracted through water or ice. The darkness before her here was dank and gritty and screamed of the unknown. She imagined the ground collapsing around her, suffocating her. . . .

"You coming?" Arief asked impatiently.

Nukilik blinked. The rancher and the orangutan and Wan were already halfway down the visible length of the passageway, beckoning her to follow. She couldn't puffin out now.

She cleared her throat and forced her feet forward.

Nukilik stayed very close to Arief's side. They turned a blind corner in the tunnel and lights flared. Sheridan laughed. He had apparently equipped the Vac-U-Pak® with floodlights.

"Pass the popcorn." Murdock hooted in the headsets. "This just gets better and better."

"Murdock, you're breaking up," Arief said.

"You're headed underground," Murdock acknowledged. "Bound to happen."

"You will start cutting out soon, the deeper we go," Wan warned. "I brought repeaters, though. So you should always have an uplink with my radio, at least."

"I'll stay on the air, then. I may need to deal with the poo collectors at some point. I think the jungle bot is getting suspicious of my marine-scented offerings."

The path descended, staying tall and wide. Nukilik noticed something unusual on the ground. "Tire tracks?" she asked.

"My golf cart, I'd wager," Sheridan said.

"Stay alert," Arief told Nuk.

Nuk was definitely feeling alert. *If Mamma could see me now, what would she say?*

"Are you sure this wasn't dug by men?" Arief asked.

"I know it's hard to believe," Sheridan said. "But this tunnel system is new. Humans didn't have anything to do with it. And look. Up ahead. I'll turn off my lights."

Wait! Don't! Nukilik thought. Her heart pounded with anxiety at the prospect of pitch blackness in this closed space. But when the rancher shut off his pack—she could still see light in the distance, down the corridor.

A minute later, they were walking beneath a strand of string lighting running along the ceiling.

"What's powering all this?" Arief asked.

"I don't rightly know," answered the rancher. "We're gonna curve steeply downward now. And then we'll come to a fork in the road. That's as far as I've ever gone."

As they descended farther, the temperature dropped, and the air grew more humid. The musty smell of freshly dug dirt clung to them as they brushed past hanging roots and sharp rock edges. They walked left and then right and then down a long, straight descent through a widening corridor.

Lone prairie dog sentinels began to pop up, standing tall along the edges of the tunnel. They watched the group walk past but did nothing. Their eyes were glazed over.

"That's not creepy," Nukilik said sarcastically. She drew close to the next rodent sentry and gave it a sniff. The prairie dog never moved. She saw no intelligence in the rodent's eyes—not even basic animal intelligence.

"Who did this to you?" she asked it.

The answer she received might as well have come from a stuffed teddy bear: silence.

As the Endangereds advanced, tunnels branched off every few yards. They were all lit by the same overhead string lighting. The prairie dog sentries followed, gathering members as they went along until there were hundreds of rodents trailing behind them.

"If we need to get out, they're blocking our way," Nukilik cautioned the others.

"You're a polar bear," said Sheridan. "Nobody's blocking your way to anything."

It was a fair point, and Nuk silently scolded herself for letting her nerves show.

"We'll never find the others this way," Arief said. "So many passages and smaller burrows."

"Should we split up?" Wangari asked, looking

between the others with green, glowing eyes.

Arief shook his head. “We need to stick together.”

They passed a wide side tunnel with overhead lighting of its own. Nukilik’s ears perked up. She thought she heard a strange cry from somewhere beyond the curving walls of the offshoot corridor.

“Did you hear that?” she asked. “Was that a ferret calling for help?”

Sheridan frowned. “Do ferrets even have a call?”

“That wasn’t a ferret,” Arief said. “It was a prairie dog trying to sound like a ferret.”

“How can you be sure?” Nukilik pressed.

“I’m not sure of anything,” Arief replied. “But that’s precisely why we need to be cautious.”

Nuk sniffed the earthy air. “I think that was Jill or Hobbs. I can smell ferret.”

“How fresh is the scent?” Wan asked. She sniffed the passageway herself. “I don’t smell ferret. I smell something else, though. Acrid. Spicy, even.”

“My nose is larger than yours. Wait here. I’ll go check it out.” Nuk turned and bounded down the corridor.

“Nukilik, stop! I don’t want us separating,” Arief insisted.

"I'll just be a minute!" Nukilik yelled back. "Come with me if you want to stay together!"

"Fine." Wangari sighed, pivoting to follow the polar bear.

Nuk veered down the side path, sniffing the air cautiously. A strange, sharp smell up ahead overpowered the ferret smell, but it wasn't anything she could place. It seemed chemical to her untrained nose. She hurried forward to investigate.

Wan suddenly cried out. "Nuk! Careful where you—"

Nukilik's foot snagged on a hard root. She pulled her leg forward—and the root came with it. It was a rope.

Nuk heard a click and a snap.

It was followed by a violent pop and a flash of light.

She turned abruptly about face as a wooden beam in the ceiling cracked down the middle and split in two.

Wangari dove into a tiny side burrow.

Nukilik caught Arief's stare of dread, and then the tunnel collapsed over her.

CHAPTER TWENTY-SIX

ARIEF

(Pongo abelii)

"Nukilik!" Arief coughed while a fog of musky earth cleared.

"Did the cave-in get her?" Sheridan asked. "Could she outrun it?"

Arief started digging at the collapsed wall of earth cutting him off from the polar bear. Nuk *had to have* reached the far passageway. Otherwise, the cave-in might have killed her. "Help me get to them!"

Sheridan put a hand on the orangutan's shoulder. "You can't dig that out with your hands. The polar bear is tough. She'll find her way. I'm more worried about your armadillo friend."

"African pangolin," Arief corrected him. "I saw her dive into a burrow. She's probably better off than Nukilik."

"They'll help each other, then. You'll see."

Arief forced himself to unball his fists.

"I say we go around," Sheridan suggested. "We'll connect up with the other passage farther down, I reckon. Then we can backtrack and find 'em both."

Arief took a deep breath. Having to backtrack to rescue Nukilik and Wan only complicated an already complicated mission. But leaving anyone behind was out of the question. "What choice do we have?" he growled to the rancher. He took another long look at the mountain of dirt separating him from his friends. "Let's go."

They hurried onward. A crowd of prairie dogs trailed them. Arief watched the critters closely. An attack felt all but certain. And then Sheridan tripped over one of the prairie dogs, falling to his hands and landing hard on the rodent. It yelped in pain and snapped at his wrist. The bite drew blood.

"Ouch! I've had enough!" Sheridan cursed, scrambling to his feet. He was clearly on edge. He fired up his U-Suck!® Vac-U-Pak® and unholstered a large tube. Thrusting the wide-diameter nozzle at the nearest statuesque prairie dog, it vanished from view, sucked off its feet with a *whoomf!*

The hose assembly convulsed. The backpack belched. The rancher laughed. Behind Sheridan, a see-through sack encased in expandable wire netting inflated. The prairie dog shot into it, stunned. It got to its feet and peered out of the balloon, rubbing its head.

The motor made Sheridan's voice choppy. "N-n-now w-w-we're g-g-etting som-m-mewhere! Lo-o-o-ok at them-m b-b-backing-g-g of-f! Ha-a-a-a-a-a!"

A second dazed prairie dog bulleted into the bubble. It gathered its bearings and huddled nervously with the first.

Sheridan smiled at Arief. "E-e-e-asy p-peasy-y-y! I can d-d-do this till the c-c-cows-s c-c-come hom-m-me."

But the situation suddenly took a turn for the worse. The colony regrouped and swarmed. Prairie dogs flung themselves at the orangutan and the human, latching on to them with sharp claws and powerful jaws.

The vacuum machine *thunk*ed and *whoosh*ed over and over, but it was of no use to Arief.

The orangutan collapsed, covered in bloodthirsty rodents.

CHAPTER TWENTY-SEVEN

WANGARI

(Phataginus tetradactyla)

Wan thought fast, squeezing into the side burrow and wrapping into a ball during the cave-in. She tasted stale dirt but waited a moment before spitting it out.

Silence.

She dared a peek through her goggles. Nothing but a wall of compacted soil to her right. And to her left: a tunnel, which narrowed quickly and would become too tight for her.

"Wan? Do you copy?" The narwhal sounded worried.

"I'm here," Wan told him. "I'm okay."

"What about Nukilik?"

"I don't know," she said, unable to hide the worry in her voice. "Give me a minute to recon."

She uncurled so that her snout and forward digging claws faced the opening. She growled, eyeing the tunnel in dismay. It was going to be a tight squeeze. But she didn't hesitate. She adjusted her goggles around her eyes and rammed herself headfirst into the dark.

Only a few feet into the crawl, her shoulders were pinned. Her utility harness pressed painfully in on her scales. She stared down into musty green blackness, fearful she could get stuck here.

"I'm digitally enhancing your feed on my end," came Murdock's reassuring voice. "Looks like the passage opens up a bit, if you can keep muscling through."

"I think I can." She muttered, battling back her panic. Three of Wan's claws on each of her front paws were long and curved, ready-made for digging into burrows to help her hunt for termites and other tasty creepy-crawlies. As a fossorial creature digging came pretty naturally to her. But living in captivity seemed to have taken away some of her confidence.

"Come on!" Murdock cheered her on. "You've got this!"

"Raaawww!" She inched forward until the tunnel expanded, and she squeezed through.

She took a deep breath of musty air. She could now crouch on her hind legs if she kept her head down.

"See? Would've been a cinch without the harness."

"You're too kind. It keeps widening," she told Murdock. "I'm going to press on."

"I'm right here with you. Unless, you know, the poo-bots start trick-or-treating."

As the tunnel grew darker, she detected something unusual, deep down below.

"Do you hear that?" Wan asked.

"No," said Murdock.

A strange thump came every several seconds. It wasn't audible so much as it was a jolt in the walls. There were faint, echoing clangs too.

She advanced. It grew colder, then warmer. The descending tunnel was suddenly lit from ahead. The gathering light felt ominous.

"Can you drop a repeater?" Murdock asked. "Your feed is flickering."

Wangari activated the next signal booster and jammed it in the wall.

"Hey! Ow!" she cried out in pain. A prairie dog was nipping at her from behind. "Stop it!"

She turned in the tight passageway, claws ready for a fight. The rodent's face glowed green in the dim light of her goggles. Wan socked the prairie dog with her balled-up claws. It fell back, dazed.

"Where'd that come from?" asked Murdock.

"Must have tunneled in from behind."

It shook its head and stared at Wan as if seeing her for the first time. There was no menace in its eyes now. It was just an animal, confused by the obstacle in its path. It bolted back up the corridor.

"You knocked some sense into it," Murdock said.

"I'm starting to wonder. . . . Maybe I actually knocked some sense *out* of it," Wangari said. "I saw its eyes. It was . . . not itself until I punched it."

The rumbling grew louder, arriving from upslope. Bits of earth rained on her head. Wan trained her sharp eyes into the green darkness. She could make out nothing but shadows—until the shadows developed neon eyes. Beady, neon eyes.

Dozens of pairs of them.

Perhaps more.

All those eyes suddenly lurched forward at once.

"Stampede!" Murdock blared. "Run!"

CHAPTER TWENTY-EIGHT

NUKILIK

(Ursus maritimus)

Nukilik couldn't move a muscle. She could hardly breathe under the weight of the collapsed dirt—but she was alive. For how much longer, though, she wasn't sure.

Why hadn't she listened to Arief instead of rushing ahead?

Nuk would have growled if she could have. But she was too frozen in place to even moan.

I wasn't good enough.

Polar bears were strong and capable creatures and

proud of it. But Nukilik had just stumbled headlong into total failure. How could she have fallen so short of the Great Realm's standards?

She had committed herself to help the Endangereds rescue Jill and Hobbs, knowing in her heart that her presence would make a difference. But she hadn't helped at all. She had only made things worse. Now she would never feel the joy of returning home, never feel the cold ice underfoot or smell the crisp Arctic air. And Mamma . . .

She would never see Mamma again.

She wanted to cry out. *Mamma!* Just saying her name would have been a comfort. But Nuk felt sure she would never see daylight again, and Mamma would never hear of all that had happened to her since they separated.

She forced herself to voice her regret. "Mamma, I'm so sorry! I just want to go home." Her mouth filled with dirt. The parched soil around her eyes wicked up her tears.

The lack of air was taking its toll.

Nuk felt herself fading into unconsciousness.

A faint sound came to her ears, providing her a surge

of adrenaline. Someone or something was nearby. *Hold on, Nuk!* She clung to the sound with the last of her hope.

It was a scratching noise!

Wan?!

Was the pangolin coming to free her? She grunted as best she could, hoping her rescuer would hear. "I'm right here!"

Finally, the dirt was brushed away from her snout. Fresh air! She wanted to laugh. It was the mustiest and stalest air she had ever known—but at least she could breathe!

She felt claws scooping away the earth around her face. Her mouth could open and close now.

"Wan? Is that you?" she asked, elated, spitting out clumps of earth.

The claws continued digging and brushing until her eyes were uncovered and she could see.

Unfortunately, the figure she saw, dimly lit from behind by string lights in the cross passage up ahead, was not Wangari.

Nukilik snarled, mustering all her pent-up strength

for a fight. She heaved under the weight of the earth pinning her down. If only she could free her front paws—but she couldn't. "Who are you? What do you want?"

"Oh, hush," said the silhouette. "Stop squirming. You're stuck and we both know it. Now, I'm on a tight schedule, but if you really want to go home, I have a proposition for you."

CHAPTER TWENTY-NINE

WANGARI

(Phataginus tetradactyla)

Wangari raced for her life, a horde of prairie dogs hot on her tail.

She came to a fork, chose a direction, and abruptly stopped.

"What are you waiting for?" cried Murdock in her ear.

"I'm gonna cave this in."

She vigorously scraped and slashed and clawed at the roof of her branch in the tunnel. Her plan worked. The ceiling collapsed. She backed out of the rubble into the clear vein beyond, shaking dirt from her shoulders and head.

The prairie dog herd rumbled past, just beyond the wall she'd formed.

"You're starting to crack up," Murdock said.

"That was a smart move, dude. It worked, didn't it?"

The narwhal laughed. "No, I mean your *signal.* Drop another booster here," he advised.

"Oh, right."

Wan spiked her second-to-last radio repeater into the ground and pressed on. She headed steadily downward. Before long, she noticed light gathering up ahead and to save power turned off her goggles' night vision feature.

"What's over there?" Murdock asked. "Seems like you're getting pretty deep for there to still be lights."

"I agree. These tunnels run much deeper than prairie dogs naturally burrow too," Wangari noted.

She could walk upright now, and the light was so bright she had to shield her eyes until her pupils readjusted. The pounding of hammers and chisels, and occasional prairie dog yips, echoed in the tunnel. In the distance, she heard the hum, perhaps, of . . . an electricity generator?

Wan started noticing a type of boxy device fastened at intervals along the ceiling, each with a small blinking green light. The boxes were too high to investigate without some serious parkour moves, but she could tell they had nothing to do with the lighting.

She approached the passage's end. A larger cavity opened beyond. She tiptoed out of the tunnel and found herself at the edge of a balcony of sorts, overlooking a narrow subterranean avenue, string-lit and teeming with activity. The tunnel walls were riddled with holes and balconies. The interior passages all seemed to connect here. More of those green blinking lights flashed in places high along the curved walls.

"It's wider than any corridor in the Ark," Wangari marveled.

Ledges carved into the walls formed walkways and stairways. Prairie dogs scurried across the pathways, hard at work. Some even dangled from ropes, wearing tiny carbide headlamps, chiseling away at the walls.

As Wan glanced at the ledge below, a metal tub filled with loose crumbles of stone wheeled along a set of narrow tracks.

"What are they doing?" Murdock asked.

"I can't even begin to guess," Wan admitted. "Wait! Murdock, are you seeing this?"

"Whoa," he confirmed. "Is that—?"

"A *golf cart.* Yes." It paraded along the earthen tube's floor. The vehicle had already passed by her position, and Wangari read a bumper sticker with an additional word Sharpied in poor penmanship next to it:

prairie DOG IS MY CO-PILOT.

Standing one on top of another, a team of prairie dogs operated the steering wheel while another team worked the gas and brakes.

The cart stopped beside a brightly lit side tunnel entrance.

A lone critter—chin up, chest puffed, and forepaws crossed—emerged from the opening in the wall.

A silver hat about the size of a teacup was perched atop its head.

Backlit and cast in shadow, Wangari squinted at the figure. "Quag," she grumbled. "That has to be him."

"By the Blue Abyss," Murdock blubbered. "That's the ugliest prairie dog I've ever seen."

DOG IS MY CO-PILOT

"I remember thinking that too, when I first saw him," said Wangari.

Quag disappeared from view as he climbed aboard the golf cart. Then he scrambled awkwardly onto the roof.

He uttered a sharp bark, and the cart started moving forward.

A blue tarp covered up the back of the flatbed. As the cart passed the side passage, a crosswind grabbed hold of the fabric and whipped it off, revealing a mesh-wire cage.

Wan and Murdock both drew in a sharp breath.

Trapped at the center of the cage were Hobbs and Jill.

CHAPTER THIRTY

ARIEF

(Pongo abelii)

Whoomf! Thunk! Whoomf! The vacuum was working, nabbing the prairie dogs one after another, thinning the horde.

But still . . . the Vac-U-Pak® wasn't enough. The overwhelming crush of critters had brought the orangutan to his knees. He cried out in pain as the rodents chomped. He pulled them off, tossed them away. But they were like boomerangs, popping straight up and hurtling themselves right back at him. Arief rose to his feet, bellowing his best Sumatran howl. He spun in a circle and shed the varmints like a lawn sprinkler. Sheridan sucked up most of them on the fly.

The wire-enmeshed balloon in the back of Sheridan's pack filled to max capacity. Sheridan slammed a button on his shoulder strap, and the sack ejected. Without missing a beat, the rancher punched another button, and a new inflatable cartridge locked into place. Prairie dogs shot into the new balloon, rapid fire. The sack expanded as it filled.

Bleeding, dazed, Arief finally flicked the last of the prairie dogs away—and Sheridan was right there to suck it up. *Thunk!*

"Y-you al-l-l r-r-right?" the rancher yelled.

"Nothing a few hundred Band-Aids can't fix." Arief sighed.

Sheridan shut off the vacuum. The tunnel was suddenly strikingly quiet. "Let's get a move on!" he yelled before realizing he was being unnecessarily loud. "They'll come at us faster than I can suck 'em up, soon enough. I've only got five balloon canisters on board."

Arief pointed at the discarded balloon full of prairie dogs. "Are they going to suffocate in there?"

Sheridan shook his head. "Naw. They'll chew

through the pouch. The wire mesh will keep them contained, though. I could add a poison gas injection and do them in," he revealed, showing Arief a switch attached to one of the pack's shoulder straps. "One of my personal modifications."

Arief's eyes widened. "No. That's the last thing we want to do."

Sheridan shrugged and clipped the small hose back into place.

They raced forward, following the overhead lights, taking a left, then a right, then another left and a downward jog. Finally, they came to a side tunnel that connected to a larger corridor. Arief hoped this passage would lead back up to where they had lost sight of Nukilik. They jogged along it, coming to an antechamber tall enough that both of them could stand fully upright.

At the back of the nook, rising three feet tall, was a round wooden door branded at the center with a *Q* inside of a larger circle.

Arief nodded, feeling hopeful for the first time since entering this labyrinth.

"Pry it open," he told the rancher. "Let's get some

answers." He had no idea what they'd find once they crouched through that door. If they were lucky, Hobbs and Jill might be in there. They could grab them and then loop back around to find Nukilik, if they weren't already too late.

Sheridan stooped and tried the handle. The round door swung open into darkness. He and Arief shared a look and ducked low to pass inside.

The aroma of dirty animals and the smell of generator gas exhaust assaulted Arief's nostrils.

"There's a light switch there," Sheridan pointed out. "Give it a flick."

Arief hit the switch, and the room lit up.

"All my stuff!" Sheridan shrieked.

It took Arief a moment to absorb the details of the den; everything about it was so elegant. The room was full of quaint southwestern décor. Candelabras with white candles and melted wax stood on a varnished, pinewood coffee table. Warm, flickering flames danced from the wicks. A small leather sofa and love seats with turquoise throw pillows were draped with Navajo blankets. The end tables were topped with polished juniper slabs. Log beams were exposed along the earthen ceiling. Several pieces of old pottery and newer Native American vases were on display. A powwow drum was tucked against one corner, and a cowhide rug lay at their feet.

"These are all your things?" Arief asked Sheridan as he glanced around for any sign of the ferrets. He started poking around. "Your cabin up top is so . . . not like this."

"That's 'cause they robbed all my good stuff out from under me!"

Arief grumbled in frustration. "No sign of Hobbs and Jill." He pointed across the room. "Let's check down that hallway."

Without warning, the lights cut out. The room was suddenly lit only by fluttering candles.

Something large and swift ran at them from the darkness, knocking Arief flat on his back. The lumbering form swiped at the rancher's bulky pack, sending it and him to the ground.

"Aliens!" Sheridan cried in dismay, terrified. "I knew it!"

It's him! Arief thought. Whoever was controlling the prairie dogs and was behind the kidnapping was here. And he was monstrously large. The orangutan sat up, suppressing a groan, and steeled himself for combat.

A roar shook the den. Arief froze in place, not believing his ears.

But through flickering candlelight his eyes confirmed it: the snarling beast on top of Sheridan was no alien.

It was Nukilik.

CHAPTER THIRTY-ONE

WANGARI

(Phataginus tetradactyla)

Wangari set off along the narrow ledge running the length of the tunnel.

"What are you going to do?" pleaded Murdock.

She whispered an answer but didn't slow. "Now's our chance! We hijack the cart, throw it in reverse. Back it out of here. No sweat."

"We?" said Murdock.

One of the light strands was plugged into the earthen ceiling. Without hesitation, Wan leaped off the ledge, reaching for the sagging lighting cable. Her claws hooked the insulated wiring and grabbed hold. Dangling high over the ground, she pulled herself up, flexed the scales on her neck, and rubbed them against the cable. The line severed with a spark. The trench went dark, lit only by the golf cart and the light seeping in from side passages.

Gravity took over, and Wangari swooped toward her target. She lifted her feet to miss brushing the ground and coiled herself into a tight ball. She landed beside Jill and Hobbs in the back of the flatbed and crouched low.

"Wan!" the ferrets cheered together in a low whisper.

"Shh."

Quag stomped in a circle on the roof. "Hey, P-dogs, what's going on? What's up with the lights? SOMEONE GET THE LIGHTS!"

"Yip! Yip! Yip!"

Wan hurriedly tried to open the wire-mesh cage, but the metal was thick and the gate was locked with an electronic pad. The cage was bolted to the flatbed and wouldn't budge. She rattled the cube in frustration. "You guys okay in there?"

Hobbs and Jill put their paws through the mesh and nodded.

Wan looked over to Quag on the roof. He tossed up his tiny arms in disgust then tapped his helmet, adjusting a dial. "What do you mean, someone severed the cable? You primitive screwheads aren't making a lick of sense."

Wangari stared in frustration toward the driver's seat. "I can't steer and pedal that at the same time without some sort of stick."

"Hold on," Murdock warned in a low, mischievous voice. "I hacked the controls."

"What?" Wan was astonished. "How?!"

"Sheridan never pass-locked the thing's fancy remote nav system. I just logged in via your signal. Here we go."

The cart peeled suddenly into reverse.

Quag and his oversized head were no match for gravity. When the cart lurched, he went tumbling down the golf cart's windshield and off the edge of the hood. His helmet came loose along the way, spinning like a top on the hood before sliding off.

Instantly, all the prairie dogs stopped what they were doing and stood stock-still, frozen in place.

Wangari jumped into the front seat, scattering the two

teams of prairie dogs that had been operating the cart.

Murdock's steering drifted, and the back bumper scraped the tunnel wall. He overcorrected, and the cart lunged into the opposite wall. The narwhal gurgled his frustration. "Your cam is my only eye, Wan. I can't see where I'm going if you glance away."

A prairie dog landed on the windshield, splayed out, dazed but unharmed.

"Ahhh!" Wangari jolted in surprise.

Murdock remotely engaged the windshield wiper. The furry thing was squeegeed out of view.

"Here, hold this, and point it straight," Wan said. She removed the small optical unit from her headset and pushed it into the ferrets' cage.

"What's going on out there?" demanded Jill from the box.

"Um, a rescue mission?" Wan told her.

Jill arched her brow. "We need a better plan."

"Murdock's driving. Don't blame me!"

Three more prairie dogs hit the windshield. The wipers quickly dispensed with them. A few more landed on the hood, slamming down against the metal and bouncing away.

"Luckily, they need a better plan too," Hobbs commented.

Wan watched the dive-bombing prairie dogs and noticed their expressions were no longer vacant. She caught a glimpse of Quag farther down the avenue, fitting that helmet back onto his banged-up noggin. "The head-gear," she said. "He's using it to control his colony!"

"Um, Wan," Jill tried.

"Step on the gas!" the pangolin cried.

Murdock did just that, and the cart shot forward and slammed into the earthen wall. Wan sailed into the cabin, hit the interior side of the windshield, and landed on the dash.

"Sorry. Trying to turn around!" Murdock said.

The prairie dogs were coming down hard now. The crazy little things were leaping from ledges, dropping from ropes. Wangari gulped. They just about had the golf cart surrounded.

"Try harder," she griped.

Twenty feet in front of the cart, Quag stood in the center of the road, illuminated in the headlights, his short arms crossed, a furious expression on his scarred face.

"Give me back my ferrets!" the critter cried. "And maybe I'll let you leave unharmed."

"What is *wrong* with that ugly prairie dog?" Wangari spat.

"Hey, Wan?" said Jill again.

Wangari poked her head out the driver's side window, just dodging a plummeting prairie dog. "What do you want with Jill and Hobbs? Where'd you get that device?"

Quag stomped his feet and rubbed his little paws together angrily. "You don't get to ask me questions! I'm afraid you've seen too much."

"Wan," Jill called over again, this time more urgently.

Quag scoffed. He reached up and adjusted the fit of his helmet, pulling it on tight. He growled a squeaky little growl and stomped his feet on the ground some more. "Attack!" he squealed.

The swarm rushed toward the golf cart.

"Cry havoc!" Quag thundered, pumping his fist. "And let slip the prairie dogs of war!"

"Murdock, are you going to drive this thing out of here or not?"

"Turn on your last repeater," he blurted into the headset. "I think we need to juice the signal."

"WAN!" Jill and Hobbs yelled together.

"What is it?" Wan snapped, searching the pockets of her utility harness for the final signal booster. "I'm dealing with a psychotic rodent right now."

The ferrets' eyes were large but not with fear. Jill pointed toward the cross-armed critter in the road. "That's what we're trying to tell you! Quag's *not* a prairie dog."

CHAPTER THIRTY-TWO

ARIEF

(Pongo abelii)

"Nukilik? Hey! Is that you? Get off me!" Murray Sheridan protested. "You're crushing me!"

The polar bear shifted her weight but kept Sheridan cornered, growling at him.

"Nuk! Stop it! It's us!" Arief jumped to all fours, thinking fast. Nuk must have hit her head during the cave-in. Maybe her hyperintelligence had been jostled somehow.

He took a step forward.

Nukilik bared her teeth. "Stay back. Don't try anything."

"Nuk, you hit your head," Arief tried explaining. "You're confused."

"No, I'm not," she insisted. "Listen, I don't want to hurt anyone. I just want this to stop. And I want to go home. I've been promised a way to get both, and I'm going to take it."

"Nukilik." Arief's voice trembled. He coughed. "We're not the enemy. We're your friends."

"I'm not working with you anymore," the polar bear declared. "I'm with Quag now." She turned her attention back to Sheridan. "All Quag wants is for *you* to give up. To leave the ranch altogether. And I'm going to help him see to it, in exchange for what I need. I'm going back to the top of the food web where I belong."

"What are you talking about?" Sheridan spat, afraid but angry. "My family's been on this land for four generations."

Nukilik's expression changed, but only slightly and only for a second. She locked eyes with Arief. "This is the simplest solution: Quag will hand over the ferrets.

You'll take them back to the Galápagos. And then he'll fly me directly home himself. Today."

"How?" Arief jeered.

"He says he has access to a plane."

"And you believe him?"

Nukilik dodged the question. "I'm sorry, Arief, but I'm done with all this silliness. It's too much."

"Nukey, baby? How's it going?" boomed an inquiring voice broadcasting loudly from unseen speakers. Arief looked around in the dim room for the source but couldn't pinpoint it. "You still with me?"

Nukilik glanced toward a darkened corner of the den. Her expression was severe and impatient. "I'm here. And Arief's here with the rancher," she told the air. "I've captured them both."

Arief saw that she was looking at a camera fastened to the wall. So, they were all being watched, and had been, possibly, all along.

"I'm dealing with them now," finished the polar bear. "You'd better hold up your end of the bargain!"

"Yeah, yeah. I keep my promises, unlike that lousy, useless ape and his train car full of circus attractions."

"What does Quag know about us?" Arief demanded of Nukilik. "What did you tell him?"

Murray Sheridan was suddenly livid—and fearless. "You animals! We shook hands! I ain't going anywhere. You take me off my own land, and I'll just find my way back. You'll have to kill me if you want my property."

Nukilik growled. She batted a paw at Murray Sheridan and sent him skidding across the dirt floor. She looked up at the camera for a brief second and then back down at the rancher. "I'm going home to my mother. I don't care about the human world. You'd better think again about what you just said, you hairless ape. Because if those are your terms"—the polar bear stepped forward and loomed over the rancher again and snarled and bared her fangs—"I accept them."

CHAPTER THIRTY-THREE

WANGARI

(Phataginus tetradactyla)

"Murdock! Hurry up!" Wangari watched helplessly as prairie dogs rained down on the golf cart.

"Any second now . . ."

Across the way, Quag spoke into a handheld radio he'd just pulled from a cradle along the wall. "Nukey, baby? How's it going? You still with me?"

Electricity shot up Wan's spine. Did she hear that right? She cast the ferrets a look. *Nukey, baby?*

Quag said something else into the radio and then turned to face his troops. The prairie dogs paused their assault to listen to their master. "We have a polar bear now!" he trumpeted, shooting his fist into the air.

Yips of triumph rippled out in a wave throughout the sea of rodents.

"Yip!"

Wan frowned. What could Quag possibly have meant? Was Nukilik captured? Was she under his control?

"No more aggression! No more oppression!" Quag angrily squeaked. He fidgeted nervously with the helmet strapped to his head. "It's the dawn of a new era!"

"Yip! Yip! Yippee!"

"Those do-gooders," Quag sneered, pointing toward the golf cart. "They want to terrorize the countryside with their ferret goons. But I won't let you be bullied!" He turned and shook his stunted tail at Wan.

With the prairie dogs in close to their leader, Wangari could plainly see now that Quag wasn't a member of their species. He was too tall and too fat. His head wasn't the right shape. His tail *was* the right length—but only because it had been cut off. Quag also moved differently than the prairie dogs; he mostly hopped on his hind legs while the others bounded on all fours.

"Resume the assault!" Quag shouted. "Don't let the ferret prisoners escape! I gotta check on things upstairs, but I'll be back. Do not fail me!" He made a quarter turn and marched into the nearest side passageway.

"Go after him!" the ferrets shouted to the pangolin.

Wan was tempted to give chase, but . . . the ferrets were still locked up. Saving them was the mission. No way she would leave them behind.

"Yip, yip, yip!" The prairie dog attack recommenced.

"Nope, nope, nope!" Murdock answered. He remotely rolled up the cabin windows and threw the golf cart into drive.

The vehicle gathered speed. Rodents flung themselves at it from all angles.

Murdock ran the cart against the walls to knock the prairie dogs loose. The ferret box stayed fastened to the flatbed, but a number of the attackers did fall away.

"If he's not a prairie dog," Wan called over to the ferrets, "then what is he?"

"No idea," Hobbs replied. "A mangled rabbit, maybe? We just know he's not part of our food web."

The vehicle turned sharply into a new section of

tunnel with no balconies, ledges, or side tunnels. An overhead assault was no longer possible, and things quieted down a bit. The floor ascended, while the ceiling pitched downward fast, and the path turned into a narrow tube lit only by the cart's lights.

"You think we're in the clear?" Wan dared to ask.

Before anyone could answer, the cart jammed to a halt, wedged against the walls of a too-tight tunnel. Wan hit the windshield as an armored ball and bounced back onto the cushioned driver's seat.

"Does that answer your question?" the narwhal teased over the comm.

Wan slipped through the cart's cracked-open rear window onto the flatbed.

"Time to bail!" Wan told the ferrets. "We need to get this cage open somehow—and fast." Opposite the electronic pin pad, the interior of the gate had a small black rectangular component. "Can you tinker from that side?" Wan asked.

"We've tried and tried," said Hobbs. "We can't tell what this is. But it's separate from the lock."

Wan wound up her tail and gave the cage a hard

swing. Not even a dent. As Hobbs and Jill poked and prodded the black casing above them, Wan tried entering 1-2-3-4-5 on the lock's number pad.

No go.

That'll never work, and there isn't time to hack it. She dug through her harness pockets, thinking.

Wan felt a rumble. Her eyes narrowed, and she peered into the dark passage they had come from. She remembered her night vision feature and turned on the power.

The prairie dog horde was galloping nearer.

"Um, gang? It's official." She ruffled her scales, fighting off a nervous chill. "We've got a rodent problem."

CHAPTER THIRTY-FOUR

ARIEF

(Pongo abelii)

Arief watched in shock as Nukilik's fangs grew closer and closer to the rancher's face. In all his long years of life, after all that had happened to him, he'd only once felt more betrayed than this and so utterly helpless to do anything about it.

Almost twenty years ago—as a young infant—he had watched his own mother and sister be murdered.

Nukilik's act of treachery left him feeling almost as empty as he had felt that day.

"Nukilik. Don't do this," he pleaded.

The polar bear turned away from her prey and gave Arief a grim sneer. "Aren't you going to stop me? I thought you were an Endangered. Where's your courage when you need it most?"

For a second, he wondered if the polar bear was genuinely asking him to get in her way.

"If you want to kill Murray," Arief said with total sincerity, "you'll have to kill me first."

"Free those prairie dogs!" shouted a new voice.

They all looked to the shadows, toward a figure hidden behind the love seat. It hopped forward under cover of darkness and kicked Sheridan's backpack. "Get them out of that bag, Nukilik! Everybody knows nature abhors a vacuum!"

This must be Quag, Arief thought.

Nukilik strode over to the Vac-U-Pak® and ripped open the sack's wire mesh with a swipe of the paw. The captured prairie dogs poured out. They fell immediately into formation along the wall and stood at attention.

The creature turned his focus to Arief. Wearing a metallic hat that looked like a bizarre teacup, he stopped, wagging his stump of a tail. He turned and looked at Arief, then gave the orangutan a knowing wink.

Arief was so confused. The critter standing before him was clearly not a prairie dog. In fact—

"Hey there, old mate!" Quag said, his tiny paws balled into tiny fists. "What's the worry? You surprised to see me alive and *not* dead? After you ABANDONED me?" The creature's gaze morphed, his eyes suddenly dancing with bitterness and fury.

They were the eyes of a quokka: a distant, miniature cousin to kangaroos.

Arief inhaled sharply. "I can't believe it." With a trembling breath, he finally dared to voice the truth. "Willie, it's you. . . . You're Willie the Wallaby."

CHAPTER THIRTY-FIVE

WANGARI

(Phataginus tetradactyla)

"If you have any tricks up your armor, now would be a good time to use them!" pleaded Hobbs.

Wan's claws brushed against her butane lighter torch.

"Stand back," she told both ferrets.

"But that'll take forever!" Hobbs argued. "The mesh is too thick to melt."

Wan shook her head. "I'm going to scorch the keypad itself. The circuitry should short and disengage the locking mechanism." She shut up and got to work, adjusting her goggles and sparking the small torch into action.

The plastic casing around the pin pad turned to goo. Wan pulled it away, plastic drooping like hot cheese from a pizza slice, and slammed her claw down on the smoldering wires within. There was a spark and a click, and the gate swung open.

"Now that's how you hack a password," Wan said with satisfaction.

A loud beep startled them all.

Hobbs scrambled out of the cage. Jill followed, but she struggled over the threshold, looking a bit dizzy and faint.

The small black contraption on the back side of the gate unexpectedly lit up with a digital display.

It was a five-minute timer—and it had just started counting down.

All along the corridor, the green lights placed at intervals suddenly flashed red.

"Detonators," Wan growled. "The box was booby-trapped! We just triggered this whole place to blow."

"Melt the timer!" Hobbs urged.

"Too late," Wan stated. "The bombs have already been triggered. We've got to hoof it!"

She heard a hiss and felt claws digging into her back.

Her scales immediately tightened, pinching off the attack. But the clawing continued. She spun around, ready to battle off a vicious prairie dog onslaught.

But instead of a rodent, she found Jill baring her canine teeth. The ferret's eyes were wild and lacked understanding.

"Jill!" Wan commanded. "Knock it off! The clock is ticking!"

"She's going feral," Hobbs protested. "We've been through too much stress."

Wan shot Jill an examining look. Her breathing had quickened. Her eyes were wide. She realized that the pressure of the situation, coupled with her pregnancy, must have activated her deepest instincts.

With an even voice, Wan tried guiding her friend through her mental fog. "We're almost out, Jill. Stay with us, now."

But the ferret snarled and sprang at the pangolin, claws and fangs exposed.

CHAPTER THIRTY-SIX

ARIEF

(Pongo abelii)

The orangutan couldn't believe he was face-to-face with his old friend, who'd been whisked away from the Ark. He'd assumed the poor animal had died like a fish out of water, maladapted, with no natural defenses in a strange new environment.

In fact, Arief had been inspired to form the Endangereds in memory of his lost companion. But here he was, back from the dead, standing before the orangutan now, a frightening sort of joy gathering in his eyes.

"I don't go by Willie anymore," Arief's old friend protested. "That was the name I was given by those human wannabe do-gooders. I'm not even technically a wallaby! I'm a quokka! Quag the Quokka!"

One of the prairie dog soldiers flipped a switch low on the wall. The overhead lights came on.

Arief saw his former companion clearly now. The chewed-up and spit-out creature was definitely his old partner—the first resident of the Ark to go hyper.

"But Willie," Arief stuttered, tripping over his racing thoughts. "You're alive! What . . . what happened to you?"

"Don't call me that!" shouted the desperate dictator, spinning in helpless circles. "My name is Quag! Quag the Quokka!"

"I thought you'd died," Arief said, grimacing. "If I'd known . . . I never would have left you behind. We were a team. I considered you a brother."

"Those useless, traitorous humans at the Ark . . . they transferred me to something called California Safari Funland. Let me tell you, I was a hot tourist attraction there, 'cause I can smile for cameras. . . ."

Quag demonstrated by posing for a pretend photo,

lifting the corners of his mouth and showing his teeth and tongue. He really did look like he was smiling. It was that quirky behavior that wild quokkas were known for, and it would have been adorable if Quag's ears weren't missing, his head wasn't all scarred, and his fur wasn't quite so patchy. Even the poor critter's tail had been bitten off—to about the length of a prairie dog's.

"What happened to you?" the orangutan asked.

"Safari Funland was just a dumb field outside of Los Angeles planted with some stupid Australian bushes—and a wild golden eagle swooped out of nowhere, snatched me up in its talons, and flew me off like I was take-out food. 'Your to-go order is ready for pick up!'" he finished sourly.

"Wi— Quag, I'm so sorry," Arief said. He looked between the quokka and Nukilik, who was watching their conversation closely. Nuk could have plucked the helmet off Quag's head, and yet she did nothing.

"I tried to keep track of you," Arief told his old friend. "But it wasn't easy back then. I saw a report from the humans. It said you died due to 'predation from above.' I was heartbroken. I thought I was all alone. The only hyper left in the world. But others like us started arriving at the Ark. We started the Endangereds in your honor, vowing to help animals in need wherever they may be. It's not too late to come back, Quag—to be a part of our team."

The polar bear growled.

Murray Sheridan, who was tinkering with the Vac-U-Pak® in the corner, looked up with disgust from what he was doing. "What?" he demanded. "You're inviting this *thief* to join you? And your polar bear just attacked me. What about our deal? What about my ranch?"

"Shut up, Mad Man Murray!" Quag spat. "I'd never join your crew. Help other animals? *Stuff* that idea! You know what I did to that golden eagle? My foot claws are as sharp as any bird's talons! I sliced it up good. Big Bird got a few good bites out of me—made *hors d'oeuvres* out of my ears and tail. But I got her back good too—and I eventually got away. She'll think twice before experimenting with foreign food again." He grinned triumphantly and adjusted his helmet. "After that, I went off the grid. Made my way here. Off to a pretty good start as far as second chances go. I realized I could use my brains to get other, more simple-minded animals to obey me. Humans have changed their environments to make their own lives easier. Why shouldn't we critters do the same?"

"And your hyperintelligence?" Arief asked. "It never faded?"

"Why would it?" Quag scoffed. "I know the secret to going hyper—and *staying* hyper."

Arief jerked. "You do?"

Nukilik leaned forward attentively.

Quag rolled his eyes. "Why would I tell you primitive screwheads what makes it work?"

"What does any of this have to do with that helmet?" Sheridan demanded, still fiddling with vacuum components. "Where'd you get *that*? And why are you building a city down here?"

Quag started laughing. "That's for me to know and you to never find out!" He scratched himself behind the stump of his ear, keeping his eyes on them, and kept talking. "When I first saw the ferret introduction happening, I knew I needed to stop it. I don't need my foot soldiers getting picked off. It's bad for morale. But then I saw that binocular-wearing pangolin and I heard her say Arief's name, and I realized who I was dealing with. I had the chance of a lifetime. To shut you down.

To tear your group apart and show you what it feels like to be hung out to dry!"

"Quag," Arief tried to explain, "you're talking like a human. Everything you're doing is destroying the natural balance. The Ways exist here in the American Southwest, just as they do for you in Australia, and for Nukilik in her Great Realm of the Arctic. The world only works if there's balance—if we coexist and take only our share."

Quag tittered meanly. "I knew you'd say that! You always were such a do-gooder. Look where *your* animal attitude has gotten us! Your family was murdered by humans. Balance? Monkey, please. Animals have been at the bottom of the pecking order for too long. Even this homesick polar bear's no match for their greed and cruelty. No thanks. Keep your lost causes to yourself."

Nukilik growled again but kept to her spot by the wall.

Arief grunted. "Your answer is to turn a blind eye and become just like the humans? How does that solve anything?"

"I wasn't put on this Earth to solve problems. I'd

rather be smart. I'd rather be rich and take what I can. Like this couch. I love this couch. Isn't it lovely? Just feel this leather! Go on, feel it!" Quag stroked the back of the couch and trilled.

"That's *my* couch, you rascal!" Sheridan yelled. He lurched forward and readied his boot to kick the quokka.

Without warning, a crackly alarm blared from an object on the coffee table, and a faint, previously unnoticed light on it switched from green to red. Quag hopped onto the table to inspect the thing. He lifted it, and Arief saw a timer display reading just under five minutes—and counting down.

"Ah, mammal!" Quag barked. "They activated the fail-safe. I wasn't sure they would. But that's how it's going to be, I guess."

"Quag," insisted Arief. "What's going on? What's that timer for?"

"Oh, you'll see." The quokka laughed. "Give it about five minutes, and you'll see." He gave a mock salute, touched his helmet, and squeezed his eyes shut, and the prairie dogs in the den marched in single file toward the dark hallway at the far end of the room. Quag set off after them, his back to the intruders. "Nukey, baby, hurry up. We've got a flight to catch."

"That's right—and allow me to punch your ticket!" Nukilik lifted a forepaw high into the air and brought it down hard—swiping the helmet from Quag's noggin. The metal fez spun like a top until Nuk slammed a fist into it, shattering it.

She immediately turned to Arief. "We have to get out of here—the whole place is set to blow."

CHAPTER THIRTY-SEVEN

WANGARI

(Phataginus tetradactyla)

Wangari batted Jill away with a powerful swipe of her armored tail. She wasn't exactly gentle about it—with Jill's claws and fangs drawn, it was obvious the ferret felt cornered and would do anything to protect herself and her kits. But Wan held back as much as she could, wanting no harm to come to her friend.

Jill hissed and squared up for another attack, her claws gripping the metal grooves in the bed of the golf cart.

"Jill! Stop!" shouted Hobbs.

An internal battle was visible in her expression. The hyper Jill was still inside the newly feral ferret. But the feral side won, and she launched herself at Wan.

The pangolin batted her away again.

Jill dug in for another go at her.

The prairie dogs were seconds away from overtaking them.

"All right, that's it," Wangari grumbled, securing the seal of her goggles around her eyes. "Hobbs, find cover!"

Sometimes an animal's best line of defense . . . is our most natural line of defense.

With a regretful grimace, Wan lifted her tail at Jill and let her anal scent glands rip.

A foul mist shot forth into the dim tunnel, hitting the wild ferret and the first row of prairie dogs about to leap onto the cart. Jill cried out in disgust, gagging. The lead prairie dogs stumbled backward. Wan glanced into the dark, readjusted her aim, and sprayed the front line of charging rodents again.

The attackers fell back, yipping in alarm. Jill collapsed in a faint.

"Holy Harvest Moon!" choked Hobbs, holding his nose. His eyes watered. "I had no idea a smell could be that bad. And I'm the one related to skunks!"

Wangari was embarrassed, but the threat had been neutralized without any lasting injuries.

She checked the countdown timer. Four minutes remained.

"We have to run," she told Hobbs. "I'll carry Jill." She snatched up the unconscious ferret with her tongue and raced awkwardly up the small corridor beyond the jammed golf cart.

As they bolted through the burrows, they found themselves turned around, even once reentering a small passage they had already been down.

"Khan oo thmell le waay aut?" asked Wan.

"I'm trying!" Hobbs said. "Stay behind me—and get back a ways. Jeez." He led like a hound, questing the ground for a scent.

"That's better. I've got a whiff of topside air!" he exclaimed. "This way." They came to a tighter passage with an upward slope.

Wan had to duck now to move forward. She thought

she might smell fresh, dry air up ahead too. But the ominous patter of prairie dog feet was right behind them as they forked into a steeper rampway.

"Qwichk! Twry ah cave-in!" suggested Wan. "It worked fow me befowr!"

Hobbs raked at the roof of the tunnel entrance, and Wan rubbed at the ceiling with her flexed scales. The roof collapsed, and they backed away from the piled dirt. A few seconds of silence followed, in which only their heavy breathing sounded in the stuffy air. Wan was beginning to believe they had lost their stalkers when the crumbly mound of fresh earth vibrated, then spat out bits of dirt, then bulged. One after another, crazed prairie dogs shouldered through the cave-in.

"They're unstoppable," marveled Hobbs.

"Wun!" the pangolin urged.

But then the prairie dogs halted in their tracks. They glanced around, their expressions full of confusion.

"What the what?" wondered Hobbs.

"Therths no thyme to figer it ouwt. Kheep moving!"

Jill stirred as Wan was yelling. The pangolin unwrapped her tongue and set the ferret down.

Jill looked up at Wangari while her eyes cleared

of their ferocity. She sat upright, ashamed. "What happened . . . ?"

Hobbs helped her along. "You went feral. But I'll explain as we run. We have to keep going."

"Feral?" she asked, leaning into a trot with the others. "I'm sorry."

"Don't apologize," said Hobbs, looking back. "I think your instincts overwhelmed your hyper abilities. The stress. And the threat. And the babies . . . We haven't been fed since before the reintro. Our instincts are built pretty deeply into us. It's not all that surprising when you think about it."

"Let's pick up the pace," Wan urged.

They gathered speed in the narrowing tunnel.

"Murdock? Do you read?" the pangolin asked into her mic.

No answer.

"He's not responding?" Hobbs asked.

"He's been quiet for a while now. Doesn't matter. Let's GO!"

They popped into a larger passage. Wan caught Arief's and Nukilik's scents and followed them. Pretty soon they found a small round door in the wall. Branded with a Circle-Q insignia, it was cracked ajar, lit from within. Something stirred in the room beyond.

"Strange things are afoot at the Circle-Q," Hobbs mused.

"I smell the others in there," noted Jill.

"Me too," Wan said. "They might not know this place is going to blow! You two head out and get as far away as you can. I'll warn the rest of the team."

"Are you sure?" Jill asked.

Wan shooed them away. "Yes. *You're* the mission. This entire region's ecosystem depends on you starting your family here. Go!"

The ferrets bounded up the corridor.

From beyond the door, Wan heard Nukilik scream in grief.

CHAPTER THIRTY-EIGHT

ARIEF

(Pongo abelii)

Nukilik smashed the helmet and turned to Arief. "We have to get out of here—the whole place is set to blow."

"WHAT! NO!" the quokka shrieked. "My hat! Why'd you do that, you big dumb bear?" He bared his teeth in fury.

"Because I'm not the dumb bear you took me for, fleabag," Nukilik roared, closing in on Quag.

"Smile for the camera!" The quokka launched himself, feet first and knife-sharp claws extended, toward his foe.

"Stop!" Arief flung himself in the way, taking the full force of the quokka's attack. He felt the claws penetrate deep into his side. The ape stumbled against the wall and collapsed with a weak grunt.

"No!" Nuk cried out. She knelt at his side. "You're bleeding!"

Arief glanced down and noticed a pool of blood gathering where he lay. A stab of fear ran up his back. He forced himself to meet Nukilik's eyes. "Don't worry about me. Get Quag."

"You got it!" whooped Sheridan. He fired up his Vac-U-Pak® and hefted the nozzle like he was holding a rifle. He detached the wand and thrust the much-wider-diameter hose assembly at the quokka.

Quag squealed in terror, tried to hop away, and got sucked into the vacuum chamber midleap.

"Got 'im!" Sheridan cheered. He reattached the plastic nozzle and swung the vacuum tube along the ground in a big arc, sucking up all of the suddenly dazed and confused wild prairie dogs huddled by the end table. They tried to fan out across the room, clasping at pottery and throw pillows and end table legs. But it was no use. Murray Sheridan collected them all.

He turned the vacuum pump's throttle down to low. "These vermin will dig themselves out of this mess. It'll all start up again! I can't take any more chances. I'm stopping them for good."

"Sheridan, wait!"

He revved the motor again, sucking up another terrified rodent bounding past his feet toward the exit door. It vanished up the tubing in a flash. Sheridan slapped a button on his shoulder strap, causing an audible hiss to rise over the other noises. The Vac-U-Pak®'s bubble sack filled with gray smoke.

Inside, Quag and the trapped prairie dogs started to cough.

Sheridan had made up his mind. "This time, I'm using poison."

CHAPTER THIRTY-NINE

NUKILIK

(Ursus maritimus)

"Nuk. You have to stop him," rasped Arief. His voice crackled. He sounded dangerously similar to Murdock speaking underwater.

Nukilik looked between her injured friend, the rancher, Quag caught in the vacuum chamber, and the countdown timer on the coffee table.

Three minutes and ticking.

Poisonous smoke eddied into the vacuum chamber—Quag and the prairie dogs were gagging inside.

"Murray! Turn that off. Listen to reason!"

Sheridan laughed. "Said the *polar bear* wearing a *flak jacket*! I may be at my wit's end, but I ain't crazy."

Nukilik was losing patience. She didn't know how much time the coughing critters had. "You can't kill them. With Quag in our custody, the ferrets and the prairie dogs will work things out naturally."

"I can't make a living off my land with these crazies coming at me all the time."

Nukilik huffed, watching Quag and the prairie dogs desperately hold their breaths while clawing against one another for low ground.

Enough talk.

She shoved Murray against the earthen wall, reached across him, and turned the backpack's motor from suck to blow.

Prairie dogs shot out of the tube rapid fire, hitting the walls, knocking over lamps. Sheridan lost control of the nozzle and was whipped around as rodents blasted out of the vacuum. Quag was pushed back into the hose but got caught where the wand narrowed. Nukilik grabbed Sheridan to steady him, chopped a paw down on the nozzle, and the quokka went flying over the sofa and struck the den's far wall, where he fell to the ground out cold.

Sheridan stumbled backward and knocked his head against a low ceiling beam. He fell over in a heap too.

Nukilik checked to see that the rancher was breathing, then reached down and shut the vacuum's motor off.

"You did it."

She whipped around, remembering Arief. His voice had been frighteningly weak. She rushed over and stooped beside him.

"I'm sorry I doubted you," Arief struggled to say. "I should have trusted you wouldn't turn on your friends."

"Arief, stay quiet," Nukilik told him. "Don't move." They nodded to each other and clasped paw to hand. Nuk fumbled through her vest with shaky paws, searching for anything of use. She found a roll of black electrical tape and wrapped Arief's torso to put pressure on his gashes. "Quag thought he was convincing me that I'd be better off joining forces with him, so I went along with it," she explained. "He knows the whole layout of this place, and I thought I'd be trapped down here forever if I didn't let him lead me back to you. I was only going to play along until we knew his plans."

"You were perfect," Arief said, his eyes growing heavy. "You make the Endangereds proud. You make me proud."

Nukilik tried to hoist the orangutan's arm around her shoulder.

Arief feebly pushed her away. "There's no time. You have to leave me and save Murray instead."

"We're the Endangereds," Nuk told his friend. "We leave no one behind."

Arief coughed faintly, and Nukilik was terrified to see that his teeth were stained with red. His eyes started to flutter.

"No. Arief! Stay awake!"

Arief's body went limp in her paws.

Nukilik's heart plummeted. Her lungs filled with stale air, and she bellowed her grief.

CHAPTER FORTY

WANGARI

(Phataginus tetradactyla)

Every twenty yards or so, the red lights on the ceiling flashed their impending doom. The entire labyrinth was on the verge of crumbling. But Nukilik's cry of agony was unmistakable. Wangari rushed through the low door to investigate.

The furniture . . . the Southwestern décor . . . Wan scarcely believed her eyes. But all of the oddities surrounding her blurred into the background when she locked her sights on Arief. His eyelids were closed shut. His body was limp. The polar bear's white fur was blotched red with the orangutan's blood.

"No," Wan whispered in sandpapery denial.

"He's gone," Nukilik mourned. "Gone. It's all my fault."

Wan gave Arief a closer look, and she was afraid Nuk might be right.

She ran forward, giving the timer on the coffee table an absent glance:

02:30

Murray Sheridan lay collapsed in the corner, stirring. "What's goin' on?" he asked weakly. "Where are we?" He got his legs underneath himself and tried to stand, remembering. "We've got to get out of here!"

Nukilik called them over. "Help me with Arief!"

Wan went to the orangutan's side. As soon as she drew close, Arief coughed up blood.

Nukilik let out a sob. "You're alive!"

The ape tried to sit up, his eyes suddenly wide open. "Oh, jeez, what's that smell?" he asked, gagging.

"I guess that's me," Wan confessed shyly.

Arief considered the pangolin with amazement. He tried to smile. "You could wake a mastodon with that stench."

"Thanks. I think."

The orangutan struggled onto three wobbly limbs while holding his tender side. He made a face. "I've lost a lot of blood. But I think you stopped the bleeding using the tape."

The red lights around the room began to flash faster and faster. Wan glanced at the room's countdown clock:

02:00

"Where'd Quag go?" Sheridan asked.

Nuk and Arief looked to a far corner of the room, as if expecting to find the rascal lying there. But the area was empty.

"He got away," Nukilik growled. "We have to find him!"

"No time," Wan urged. "We need to head for the surface before it's too late."

"He must have an escape route," Sheridan said. He

marched over to the hallway and tried the doors that were back there. They were locked.

"I'm too weak," Arief said, propping himself against the wall. "I can't make it."

"And I'm a polar bear," Nukilik declared. "Shut up, hop on, and hold tight."

"How am I supposed to ride you?" Arief grunted, favoring his side.

"Any which way but loose," Wangari barked. "But move it!"

Sheridan helped Arief to mount Nukilik's back, and they ducked out of the den.

"If we double back to the next passage," Nukilik explained, "that should lead us to the way out. It's a straight shot from there!"

The red detonator lights pulsed faster and faster.

Nukilik led the way at a gallop. The group kept up. A flood of prairie dogs joined the mass stampede toward the surface. Their eyes were dark but clear, wild but under their own control.

Along the way, they came across Sheridan's first discarded sack of trapped prairie dogs and cut them loose. The grateful rodents launched into a full sprint beside everyone else, yipping and barking their relief. "We're free!"

Before long, Wan detected natural sunlight up ahead.

Nukilik and Arief were first out of the tunnel. Then Sheridan, alongside countless agitated prairie dogs.

Wangari knew the jolt was coming—but it was still frightening when it hit. A shock wave. Beyond scale. It registered in her mind only as profound confusion. Then she felt her stomach free-fall sickeningly. The earth around her closed in.

After a moment—or maybe it was longer—Wan's mind became aware again.

Pure darkness.

Heavy earth.

She was curled tight into a ball, unable to stretch out.

"Wan! Do you copy?"

The transmission was a little garbled. It took the pangolin a second to realize this was simply because an underwater narwhal was speaking in her ear.

"I hear you!" she mumbled. She tried to assess her situation, still recalling memories of the last several minutes. She couldn't even turn her head. *Oh, yeah: I'm buried somewhere in Utah, Colorado, Arizona, or New Mexico.* "I wouldn't exactly characterize myself as being okay but—"

"Sorry I was checked out for so long. Those dumb poo-bots came around demanding Nukilik's tribute. You know how they are. I had to give 'em something. Anyway, did I miss anything?"

Wangari managed a muffled laugh. "Just pinpoint my position and send it over to the others, will you?"

"Gotcha, buddy. Hang in there. I have your coordinates."

Wangari waited. Her breathing was steady. She knew she'd be okay. The Endangereds were on their way.

CHAPTER FORTY-ONE

ARIEF

(Pongo abelii)

Back at the ranch, *Red Tail* was parked beside Murray Sheridan's cabin. A ramp descended along the side of the hull. Standing on it as it lowered were a scruffy polar bear, a chewed-up orangutan, a beach ball–sized walking artichoke with a tail, and a very pregnant ferret and her mate.

Arief limped his way to the porch while the other Endangereds readied themselves for departure. Arief took a seat in the rocking chair and allowed Wan to tend to his wounds.

"Look at you!" Wangari scooped a bit of dirt out of her ear with a claw as she examined the ape. "These bandages will have to be changed a couple times before we get back to HQ. You're going to need antibiotics too. Dr. Fellows is going to flip out if she corners you before you're healed. She'll want to know why something thought you were a buffet."

"I'll make sure she doesn't get too close for a while," Arief promised.

He thought about the vet. Murdock had confirmed that Dr. Fellows was heading back to the Galápagos. Knowing the doctor as well as he did, Arief was sure she'd be kicking herself, thinking she'd failed the ferrets. But the Endangereds would make sure that the remote wildlife cameras would snap a few shots of Hobbs and Jill—and their kits—doing well in their new wild home.

Quag's detonators had been distributed pretty equally in a grid for a mile in every direction. Everything on the landscape, from the infrequent buildings and the roads to the bushes and trees and telephone poles—it all looked like a tabletop after a tablecloth-pulling magic trick: slightly off-kilter but mostly upright and generally okay.

The humans were bound to conclude they had been in a localized earthquake. With any luck, Dr. Fellows and Officer Nez would assume yesterday's strange prairie dog behavior had something to do with the peculiar, documented ability of some animals to sense tremors and then grow anxious before seismic events.

Nukilik came up the steps and took a seat beside Arief and Wan after removing the stuffed jackrabbit from the second rocking chair. She carefully placed it on the end table and gave it a hard glance. "Poor fellow. What a world—this critter ends up stuffed and Quag lives to see another day. He can't have gotten far. I have half a mind to hunt him down while the trail is hot."

"I failed Quag." Arief gulped down a lump in his throat. "He's my fault. I didn't mean to, but I created a monster."

"This wasn't your fault, Arief," Wan argued. "You can't blame yourself."

Arief stared out into the distance. He nodded to make Wan happy, but he still felt responsible.

"Don't worry about Quag for now," Murdock said, trying to lift the mood. Arief put a finger to his ear, adjusting a headset dial. "We'll know it if he turns up again. Here, or anywhere he runs to. And this time we'll be ready."

Wangari nodded. "Right now, we have more important matters to wrap up." She gestured to the rancher, who had just parked his truck next to *Red Tail* and was approaching on foot. "Hobbs and Jill won't succeed out here without Murray's help."

Sheridan stepped up onto the porch. He took off his cowboy hat and scratched the top of his head. "Well, that about settles it, don't it? You held up your end of the bargain best you could, I suppose. I didn't get none of my stuff back, but at least that crazy helmet got crushed. I can start over, I guess. Plant some crops finally. Maybe get a couple head of cattle to start."

He handed Nukilik an old sun-bleached bone he'd found out on the range. The polar bear accepted it with a laugh and started grinding on it.

"What about the ferrets?" Arief asked him directly. Everyone looked down at Jill and Hobbs, who were rummaging through the sage, inspecting some old burrows. "They'd like to stay here. Jill is just about ready to have her kits. She and Hobbs really want them born in the wild."

"What about their smarts? They gonna start harassing me like that Quag feller did?"

"They just want to be where they belong. They want to live natural lives," Wan assured him. "And if Quag's dumb enough to return, you just give us a ring."

"Are you willing to watch out for them, for the ferrets?" the polar bear pressed, her gaze hard-set. "They need more than your blessing. They're going to need your protection."

Sheridan hesitated. "Call me enviro-curious," he said. "Do the P-dogs have to come with the territory?"

"It's all about balance, Murray," Arief reiterated. "The prairie dogs are actually what we call a keystone species. They're habitat builders. A lot of wildlife—and even plants—count on them out here for a healthy environment."

Sheridan slowly nodded. He spit in his palm and thrust his hand out to the ape. Taken aback by the barbaric gesture, Arief extended his tired and sore arm anyway.

"We'll make it work, I guess," Sheridan vowed.

And there it is, Arief thought with an immense feeling of satisfaction—and hopefulness. *It all starts with a conversation between friends.*

"It's thoughtful landowners like you that can really make a difference," Arief told the human. "Thank you."

"I guess that's it for us," Nukilik announced, giving her new bone a chomp. "We should go. Arief needs access to the Ark's medicine before infections start doing him in."

The Endangereds and the rancher and the newly reintroduced ferrets said their goodbyes. It was difficult for the team members to bid Hobbs and Jill farewell. Tears were shed throughout the team. Jill expressed her gratitude to everyone, but a wild excitement was creeping over her features. She bounded away without looking back at the group, impatient to continue house hunting among the available prairie dog burrows.

"Thank you so much for everything," Hobbs told them, ready to run off into the sage to be with his mate.

"We'll keep an eye on you for a while," Arief promised. "And Dr. Fellows will see that you're doing okay. Maybe Sheridan can report in to us occasionally. But we know you'll do great out here."

"Live your best wild lives," Nukilik told them. "Do it for the rest of us. You hear me?"

"Aren't you next, Nukilik?" Hobbs asked.

Nukilik's eyes filled with fresh tears. She blinked them away, unashamed, looking between everybody. Her gaze settled on Arief. "I want to find my mother," she began. "I want to know that she's okay, and I want *her* to know that *I'm* okay. But most of all . . . I want her to know . . . that I've found my purpose."

"We'll get you home, Nuk," Arief said, nodding. "We'll redeploy as soon as we can resupply."

"No. I don't think you're hearing me." The young polar bear cleared her throat. She looked hard at the orangutan. "I have a home now. I have a new family. And I have a job to do."

For a long moment, the porch was silent.

Nuk cleared her gravelly throat again, her tone lifting. "We're making a promise to all of our endangered friends," she declared. A hopeful grin spread across her features. "To any animal or species that's in trouble—if you're threatened, vulnerable, endangered, extinct in the wild: if you have a problem, if no one else can help . . . you can count on the Endangereds."

The team slowly filed back into *Red Tail*. Nukilik stood at the open door, looking out at the frolicking ferrets. She asked Arief, "You sure Hobbs and Jill and their family are going to be okay out here?"

Arief answered with a nod. "They'll be okay, Nuk. I think we made a positive difference this time. And I think we'll do it again."

"Yes," Nukilik vowed. "For as long as it takes."

The polar bear pointed at something stuck to the inside of the door. "Hey, what's this?"

Arief drew nearer, giving the unfamiliar white object a serious inspection. It kind of looked like a smoke detector, but he didn't remember ever seeing it before. "I have no idea," he admitted. "But I don't think it belongs onboard."

"It doesn't," confirmed Murdock, watching through *Red Tail*'s onboard dash camera.

"A tracker?" asked Wan, stepping over to inspect it.

"I just did a quick rewind of the dash's log," grumbled Murdock. "A prairie dog put it there shortly after you guys drove off in Sheridan's truck. Quag must have ordered for it to be put there."

Arief felt a cold chill. "What should we do with it?" he wondered.

“Easy,” said Nukilik. She swiped it to the floor and stepped on it, crushing it.

“Whoa! Hey! Maybe next time just *turn it off*?” complained Murdock. “We could have studied it!”

Nukilik gave her weathered bone a pensive turn. “I should have thought that through more.”

Murdock offered a low gurgle of resignation. “Keep it anyway,” he suggested. “We can repair it.”

But before anyone could pick it up, the device started smoking and burst into flames, as if the polar bear had triggered a self-destruct function.

Lightning quick, Wan slid feet first and kicked the smoldering ruin out of the aircraft. She jumped to the ground and buried it in dirt. “So much for following *that* lead.” She sighed.

“Get back here, you guys,” Murdock griped. “I’m telling you, if these poo-bots get another half-ton delivery of smelly fish poop for their bellies, they’re going to revolt.”

“Sounds revolting,” said Arief.

Red Tail’s propellers started to spin. Arief lingered at the open door. He watched as Jill darted through the grass, chasing a prairie dog into the distance. A chorus of yips rose throughout the countryside, followed by an approving whoop from the rancher rocking on his porch. Jill looked up from the sage, poised on her hind legs, searching for her partner. She gave Arief one last knowing wink then called out to her mate with a wild glint in her eyes.

"Lunch is on!" she shouted to Hobbs over the gathering noise of the engines. "Come and get it!"

THE END*

**No humans were harmed in the making of this adventure.*

EPILOGUE

"Hey, what's this?"

"I have no idea. But I don't think it belongs onboard."

"It doesn't."

"A tracker?"

"I just did a quick rewind of the dash's log. A prairie dog put it there shortly after you guys drove off in Sheridan's truck. Quag must have ordered for it to be put there."

"What should we do with it?"

"Easy."

The video feed's perspective quickly changed as the recording device fell to the ground. A polar bear foot filled the screen, and then the image and the audio cut out.

The figure sitting at the desk leaned back and huffed. "Well, that didn't work like we planned."

"They're far too close to the truth already," said a monitor lizard standing upright just behind the figure's tall-backed chair.

"They're wising up fast." The owner of the voice reached out and petted a calico cat purring on top of the desk in front of him. "But isn't that the point? I think I'll let them stumble around some more, for the time being, and see what kind of intel they surface. Munson, can you pull me up the list of syndicates we're currently selling Neuroflexicin to?"

"Yes, m'lord," hissed the monitor lizard, testing the air with his long tongue. "What about Quag, m'lord? We've lost track of him."

"Good riddance. *Quag.*" He scoffed at the name. "It was a mistake to partner with the quokka. He took his personal ambitions too far. His passions run deep—I'll give him that. On second thought, maybe we'll use him again if he turns up." He chuckled mirthlessly. "But still continue the larger search, will you, Munson? And double-check that our other test populations have sufficient supplies to proceed. We should warn them that the Endangereds have a taste for meddling."

"Yes, m'lord."

"Now, leave me. You and your disgusting, flapping tongue both. Go monitor something. Or whatever it is you do."

"Yes, m'lord." Munson dropped to all fours and slunk out of the office.

M'lord—it was a title he rather appreciated—reached out a lanky arm covered in coarse hair. He petted the simple-minded house cat. The non-brainy animal purred its misguided gratitude and rolled its cheeks to match its master's scratching.

"It won't be long now, Cookie"—he spoke in soothing tones to the domesticated little feline—"before the humans learn they're no longer at the top of the pecking order. Isn't that right?"

The happy-go-lucky cat agreed with a delighted meow.

ACKNOWLEDGEMENTS

First, I would like to thank David Linker, executive editor at Harper. After only a few short calls between us, he distilled my hope of creating a story that could inspire young people into the idea that became *The Endangereds*. This book would not exist without his literary brilliance. Camille Kellogg also played an especially important role in realizing the potential of this book and working tirelessly to make it a reality. I am also incredibly grateful to my agent Cait Hoyt; she saw the potential of a partnership with HarperCollins and was instrumental in making this project happen.

I would like to thank my co-author Austin Aslan for his thoughtfulness, creativity, and generosity of spirit. I could not have asked for a more talented and passionate co-author. To my team at EarthEcho International, thank you for all your support and suggestions, especially

Mia DeMezza, who has put up with me for fourteen years and has been instrumental in growing our little dream of an organization into a global force that is building a youth movement for the ocean. I would like to thank my amazing wife, Ashlan, for all the nights she spent up with me thinking through ideas for the book and reading draft after draft, providing invaluable insight, creativity and inspiration. Finally, I would like to thank my mother Jan, who as a single mother raised my sister Alexandra and me, instilling in us a lifelong belief that each and every one of us has a responsibility to do the best we can to build a better world for people and the planet. This book is a result of that belief and it exists because of what she continues to inspire in me every day.

—Philippe Cousteau

I am eternally indebted to Philippe and our editor, David Linker, for extending me the invitation to partner on this project. I'll never forget how excited and eager I was when *The Endangereds* first came across my radar. Nukilik's mom mentions that Nuk was created with great purpose in mind. I've always aspired to bring purpose to my writing and my stories, and I recognized immediately the ambitious purposefulness of this series. I share Philippe's deep passion for global biodiversity and the integral connection between ecosystem health and human well-being. I am grateful beyond words for the opportunity to pour my professional background and my personal heart and soul and my own rooted sense of great purpose into this endeavor. And of course, none of those things would be as strong as they are without the influence of my wife and two children. Clare, so much of my love for the natural world stems from your vocation as a PhD in conservation biology, and the inexhaustible passion and expertise you bring to your mission. Your work takes our family outdoors and to exotic locales all the time, and the ways in which those experiences shape the values of our children, who will carry the conservation torch forward, are beyond priceless. I would like to give shout-outs to my agent Paul Lucas and Camille Kellogg at HarperCollins for their influence on the story, and also thank author and friend Ryan Dalton for his critical feedback early during the drafting process. David Linker, I can't help but mention you twice because you deserve the extra credit for guiding the narrative along and putting up with all sorts of wild (or is the term feral?) ideas along the way. Finally, I want to express my awe and gratitude to James Madsen, the incredibly talented illustrator who has portrayed the Endangereds with such vivid detail and depth of expression. It was truly a delight to watch you bring these characters and settings to life.

—Austin Aslan

ABOUT THE ANIMALS

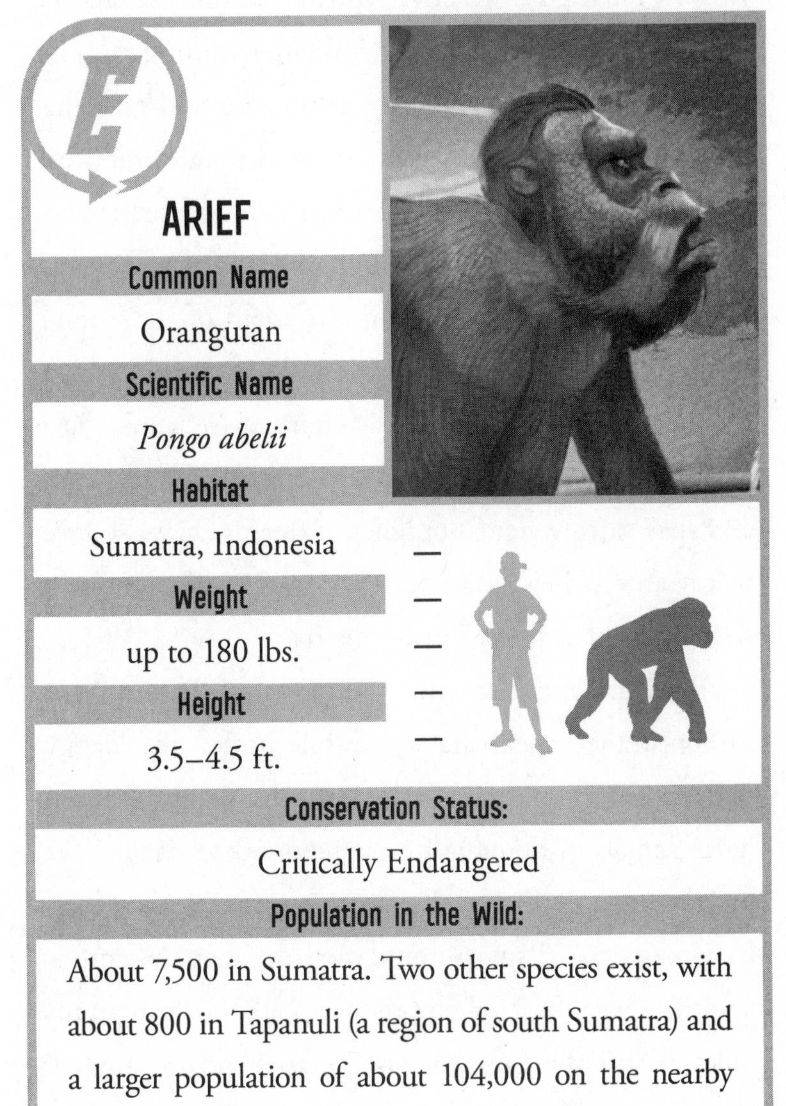

ARIEF

Common Name

Orangutan

Scientific Name

Pongo abelii

Habitat

Sumatra, Indonesia

Weight

up to 180 lbs.

Height

3.5–4.5 ft.

Conservation Status:

Critically Endangered

Population in the Wild:

About 7,500 in Sumatra. Two other species exist, with about 800 in Tapanuli (a region of south Sumatra) and a larger population of about 104,000 on the nearby island of Borneo.

LEARN MORE:

Known for their distinctive red fur, orangutans are the largest arboreal (tree living) mammal, spending most of their time in trees. Long, powerful arms and grasping hands and feet allow them to move through branches. Did you know that these great apes are very smart and share more than 90% of our human genes? How cool is that? The name orangutan means "man of the forest" in the Malay language. In the lowland forests in which they reside, orangutans live solitary existences. They feast on wild fruits like lychees, mangosteens, and figs, and they slurp water from holes in trees. They also love to eat ants. They make nests in trees of vegetation to sleep at night and rest during the day.

Bornean and Sumatran orangutans differ a little in appearance and behavior. While both have shaggy reddish fur, Sumatran orangutans have longer facial hair. Sumatran orangutans are reported to have closer social bonds than their Bornean cousins. Both species have experienced sharp population declines. A century ago there were probably more than 230,000 orangutans in total, but the Bornean orangutan is now estimated at about 104,700 based on updated geographic range

(Endangered) and the Sumatran about 7,500 (Critically Endangered). They are threatened by deforestation and illegal capture for the wildlife trade.

A third species of orangutan was announced in November 2017. With no more than 800 individuals in existence, the Tapanuli (an isolated region in southern Sumatra) orangutan is the most endangered of all great apes.

WHAT CAN YOU DO TO HELP ORANGUTANS?

Orangutans are critically endangered animals, and only live in two places: in the countries of Borneo and Sumatra. Orangutans are threatened by destruction to their habitat. Their rainforest homes are being destroyed by deforestation—the cutting down of large amounts of trees at one time. Because rainforests need to be protected to protect orangutans, when your family buys things made of wood, you can look for responsibly sourced wood products that guarantee the wood product you are buying wasn't made from deforested trees.

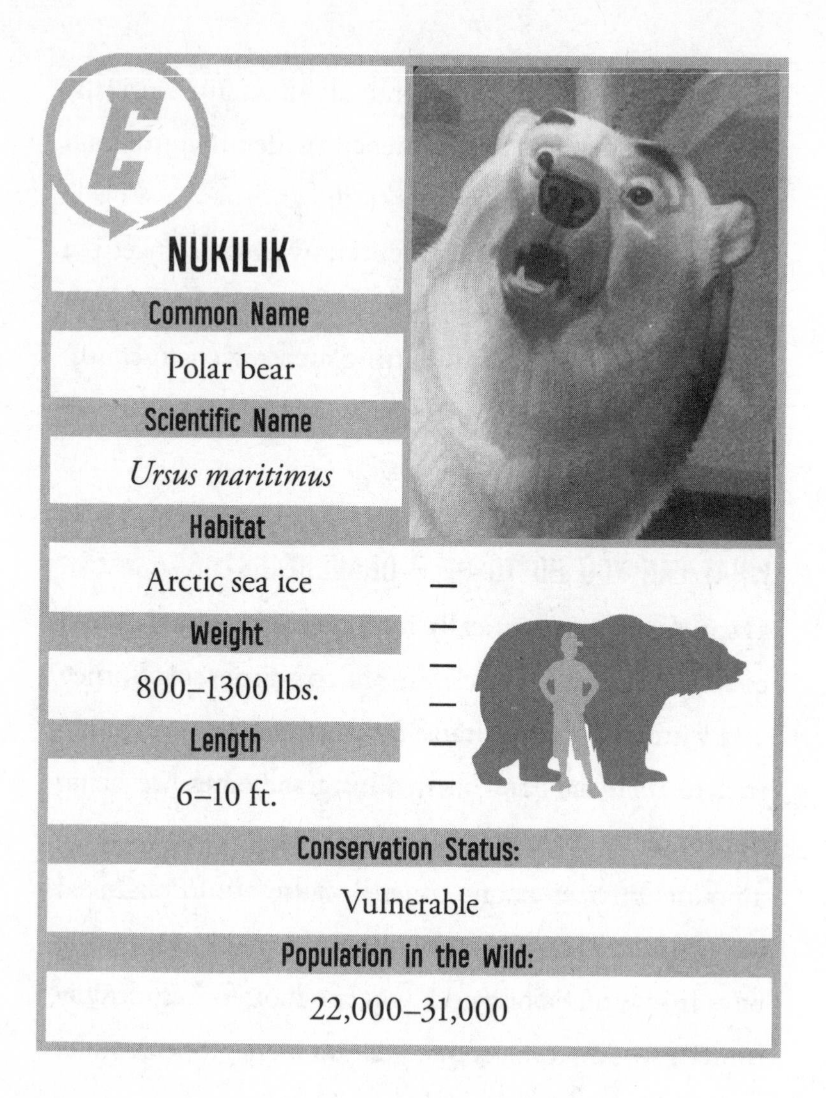

LEARN MORE:

Polar bears are one of the most important mammals in the Arctic and are vital to the health of that ecosystem.

They are known for their water-repellant fur coat that appears white but is actually made up of transparent hollow hairs. Did you know that polar bears have black skin under their white fur? It helps them absorb the heat from the sun! Polar bears spend over 50% of their time hunting for food by waiting on the ice for seals to come up for air.

Polar bears are classified as marine mammals because they spend most of their lives on the sea ice of the Arctic Ocean. They have a thick layer of body fat and a water-repellant coat that insulates them from the cold air and water. Considered talented swimmers, they can sustain a pace of six miles per hour by paddling with their front paws and holding their hind legs flat like a rudder.

Because of ongoing and potential loss of their sea ice habitat resulting from climate change, polar bears were listed as a threatened species in the US under the Endangered Species Act in May 2008.

WHAT CAN YOU DO TO HELP POLAR BEARS?

What we do in our daily lives impacts polar bears because of our connection to Earth's ecosystem. What we eat, how we use electricity, and how we travel effects the climate, which affects the Arctic ice habitat. Talk to your family, friends, and others in your community about making small changes in their daily routines. For example, waste less food at dinner, bike or walk to school, turn off the lights in your home when you leave a room—these are all small ways to make a big impact. You have the power to be a leader in your community just like the Endangereds.

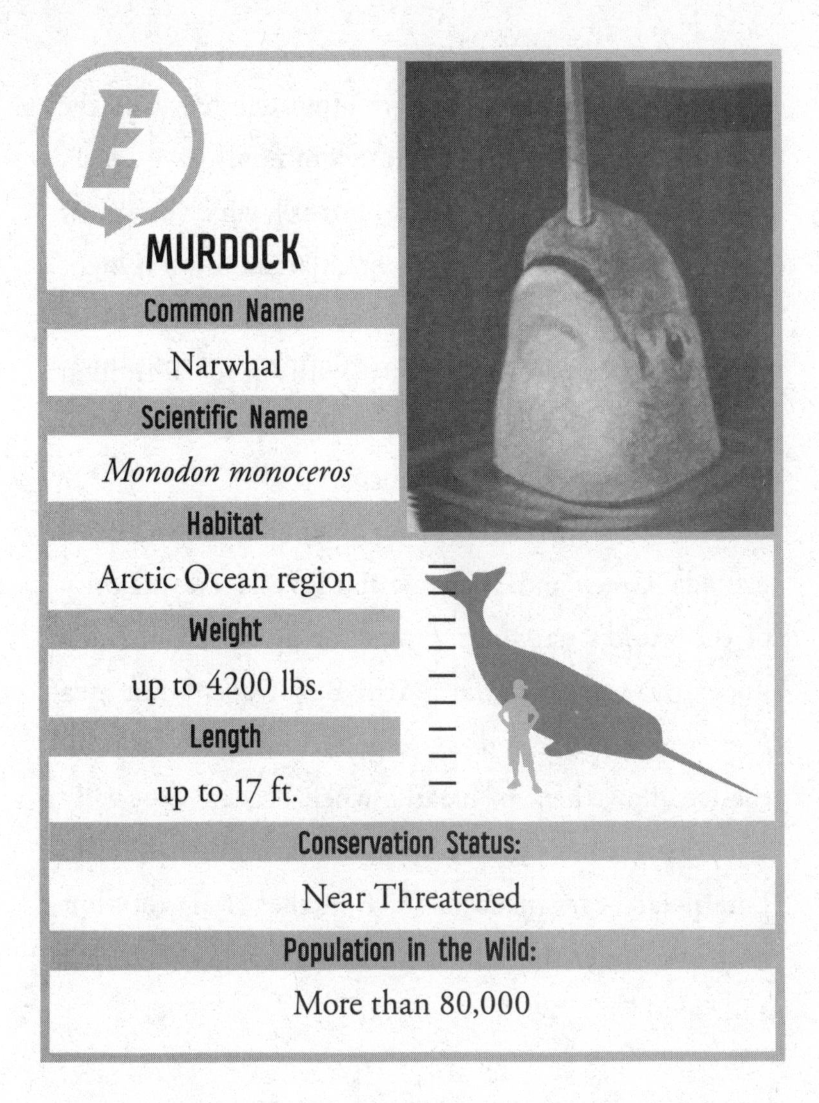

LEARN MORE:

The narwhal looks like a cross between a whale and a unicorn with its long, spiraled tusk jutting from its head. For that reason, they are often referred to as the "unicorn of the sea." Males most commonly have a tusk, and some may even have two. The tusk, which can grow as long as 10 feet, is actually an enlarged tooth. Ongoing research by WWF and collaborators indicates that the tusk has sensory capability, with up to 10 million nerve endings inside. The tusk may also play a role in the ways males exert dominance.

Narwhals spend their lives in the Arctic waters of Canada, Greenland, Norway, and Russia. The majority of the world's narwhals winter for up to five months under the sea ice in the Baffin Bay–Davis Strait area (between Canada and western Greenland). Cracks in the ice allow them to breathe when needed, especially after dives, which can be up to a mile and a half deep. Like polar bears, narwhals live in the Arctic too, but they live under the water and like to eat cod, shrimp, and squid.

WHAT CAN YOU DO TO HELP NARWHALS?

Just like with polar bears, what we do in our daily lives impacts narwhals because of our connection to Earth's ecosystem. What we eat, how we use electricity, and how we travel affects the climate, which affects the Arctic ice habitat. Talk to your family, friends, and others in your community about making small changes in their daily routines. For example, waste less food at dinner, bike or walk to school, turn off the lights in your home when you leave a room—these are all small ways to make a big impact. You have the power to be a leader in your community just like the Endangereds.

LEARN MORE:

Black-footed ferrets are known as the "masked bandits" of North America. They are nocturnal, meaning they are mostly active at night. And they are also fossorial, meaning they mostly live underground. They are long and slender, which enables them to move very easily underground in prairie dog burrows.

Once thought to be globally extinct, black-footed ferrets are making a comeback. For the last thirty years, concerted efforts from many state and federal agencies, zoos, Native American tribes, conservation organizations, and private landowners have given black-footed ferrets a second chance for survival. Today, recovery efforts have helped restore the black-footed ferret population to nearly 300 animals across North America. Although great strides have been made to recover the black-footed ferret, habitat loss and disease remain key threats to this highly endangered species.

WHAT CAN YOU DO TO HELP BLACK-FOOTED FERRETS?

Black-footed ferrets were once thought to be extinct, but due to efforts by many state and federal agencies, zoos, Native American tribes, and conservation organizations like World Wildlife Fund, they are making a comeback. The reintroduction of black-footed ferrets into prairie dog colonies—like the storyline of Jill and

Hobbs—is one of the many methods that are helping. But the work to save them is not over. You can join with friends and family and call your member of Congress to tell them you support the Endangered Species Act, one of the most effective laws to protect at-risk species—like the black-footed ferret—from extinction.

LEARN MORE:

Did you know the black bellied pangolin is also called the long-tailed pangolin because its tail can be twice as long as its body! They live in central Africa and spend most of their time in trees. But they are only one of 8 different species of pangolin found in Africa and Asia.

Many people think pangolins are reptiles due to their scales, but pangolins are actually mammals and they are the only mammals covered fully in scales. Pangolins use their scales to protect themselves. If they feel threatened, they immediately curl up into a tight ball and use their sharp tails to defend themselves. Pangolins live in Asia and Africa and eat ants and termites!

Pangolins are solitary, primarily nocturnal (they are active at night) animals. Also called scaly anteaters because of their preferred diet, all species of pangolins are increasingly victims of illegal wildlife crime—mainly in Asia and in growing amounts in Africa—for their meat and scales. There is also growing demand in the United States for pangolin leathers, which are used to make products like boots and belts.

WHAT CAN YOU DO TO HELP PANGOLINS?

Sadly, pangolins are one of the most trafficked (meaning stolen or traded illegally) mammals in the world. Some people think their meat is special to eat, and others also steal their scales to to make traditional medicines. You can learn more about how trafficking affects pangolins and other animals by visiting World Wildlife Fund's website. Tell your friends and family not to buy live animals or products made from animal parts when you go on vacation.

ABOUT WORLD WILDLIFE FUND (WWF)

WWF's work is focused on how we are all connected to the natural world around us—and to each other. Its efforts put people at the center, and they work on six key areas: protecting wildlife (like the animals in this book!), preserving and restoring critical habitats like forests, oceans, freshwater rivers and streams, and preventing the worst threats to our planet like climate change and irresponsible food production. All these issues are connected. And you can help WWF protect the planet and its natural resources.

ABOUT EARTHECHO INTERNATIONAL

We hope that you have enjoyed *The Endangereds*. It is inspired by my deeply rooted belief that youth hold the key to building a better, more sustainable world and it is a part of my life-long dedication to empowering young people to recognize that power within themselves.

In the spirit of that idea, I wanted to share with you a little bit about my organization EarthEcho International, a global non-profit I founded fifteen years ago to give young people the knowledge and tools to create a thriving water planet.

All over the world, EarthEcho works with young people just like you, youth who care about animals and the environment and are passionate about making the world a better place. We use adventure, storytelling, and education to empower and inspire young people worldwide to act now for a sustainable future.

If you loved *The Endangereds* and want to help the world, just like Arief and his team, EarthEcho is here to help.

We are building a movement of young people who care about the environment with a specific focus on the ocean, because whether you live along the coast or not, the ocean is the life support system of this planet. It regulates our climate (particularly important to Nuk's home), provides food to billions of people, and is a source of wonder and excitement for us all.

At EarthEcho, we have lots of different programs that are designed to help you learn about and take action to protect the environment in your very own communities. Our youth leaders have passed laws, raised critical funds, started movements to protect land, founded successful businesses that help people and the planet, and so much more.

I know it seems like there is a lot of bad news about the environment these days, but I also know that there is tremendous hope. I have been all over the world and it is the optimism and determination that I see on the faces of young people just like you that reminds me of how much good there is in the world. There is a movement of young people who recognize that when we come together, just like Nuk, Arief, Wan, and Murdock did, there is nothing that we cannot achieve, no problem we cannot overcome, and no one who can stop us from building a better world.

So join us and become a part of the movement at www.earthecho.org.

Philippe Cousteau,
Founder, EarthEcho International